TERMINATE
RETRIBUTION

TERMINATE
RETRIBUTION

NATASHA DEEN

ORCA BOOK PUBLISHERS

Library and Archives Canada Cataloguing in Publication

Deen, Natasha, author
Terminate / Natasha Deen.
(Retribution)

Issued in print and electronic formats.
ISBN 978-1-4598-1462-2 (paperback).—ISBN 978-1-4598-1463-9 (pdf).—
ISBN 978-1-4598-1464-6 (epub)

I. Title.

PS8607.E444T47 2017   jC813'.6   C2016-904582-x
C2016-904583-8

First published in the United States, 2017
Library of Congress Control Number: 2016950089

Summary: In this next installment of the high-interest Retribution series,
Jo and her friends team up again to figure out why so many homeless
teens are ending up in the city morgue.

*Orca Book Publishers is dedicated to preserving the environment and has
printed this book on Forest Stewardship Council® certified paper.*

Orca Book Publishers gratefully acknowledges the support for its publishing
programs provided by the following agencies: the Government of Canada
through the Canada Book Fund and the Canada Council for the Arts,
and the Province of British Columbia through the BC Arts Council
and the Book Publishing Tax Credit.

Cover image by Getty Images
Author photo by Curtis Comeau

ORCA BOOK PUBLISHERS
www.orcabook.com

Printed and bound in Canada.

20 19 18 17 • 4 3 2 1

For Sven

ter·mi·nate (ˈtər-mə-nāt)
    verb
to end in a particular way or at a particular
place; to cause (something) to end

ONE

When it came to the low-lifes of the world, I was Bad Santa. The criminals better not run, and they better not cry. I was coming to get them, and they knew why.

Last time they had been in my sights, it was so I could avenge my family's murder. This time it was to find a friend who had fallen into darkness. I was going to bring her back to the light. If that cost a couple of bad guys their freedom, a few teeth and some broken bones, I was fine with that.

And I had a no-fail plan. At least, that's what I told myself as I headed into the East Hastings Community Kitchen.

I got three steps in before Clem's rock-and-gravel voice sounded my way. "I'm getting awful tired of telling you to take off those sunglasses whenever you come in here."

Some people say hello when they see each other. Not Clem and me. That would be too touchy-feely. For us, it was hound-dogging each other. I wore sunglasses to tweak him. He called me out on it to show he had noticed.

Even if it wasn't routine, Clem had a superhero ability to see 360 degrees at once. It was one of the reasons he had been considered one of the best snipers the armed forces had ever known. He was a military guy, all the way. Respect. Loyalty. Teamwork.

In a lot of ways, I looked up to him. Wanted to have the same kind of integrity he did. But there was a danger in caring for people and caring about those around you. Death and loss. In his case, he had lost half his troop and one of his legs.

The last few weeks I had been obsessing about loss. Because now I had a team too. Raven, who was fast becoming a sister from a different mister. Bentley, the smart-aleck brother from another mother. And Jace, who called up too many yet-to-be-named feelings for me to ever feel safe around him.

"Sunglasses," Clem repeated. "Are you deaf?"

"You got your head down," I said. "No way you know if I'm wearing sunglasses or not." I spun left and walked to where he stood by one of the food counters. I waited for the next line in our routine.

As usual, he kept his gaze on the clipboard in his hands. "I got a sixth sense."

I pushed the sunglasses onto my head. My phone buzzed, but I ignored it. I knew who was on the line. Raven. She'd been riding me about registering at her school. I appreciated her mama-hen routine, but until I found Amanda, I didn't have time for anything else.

3

Clem looked up, took in the fading bruises from my run-in with Meena and the Vëllazëri street gang a few weeks back. He stood and stretched his beefy neck. "Better-looking every time I see you."

"You're a laugh a minute."

"You're alive." Silence. "Good—I had fifty bucks riding on whether you'd survive whatever stupid scheme you'd hatched. Now I can take myself to The Keg for dinner."

"Of course I survived. I know better than to come between you and a steak dinner."

Clem slapped me on the back with his clipboard. I winced.

"You know I'm still healing, right?"

"Next time, duck," he said.

"You giving boxing advice or telling me your dinner plans for next week?" I asked.

He almost smiled. "You here to work or just exercise your jawbone?"

"Unlike you, I can do two things at once."

"Then stock the shelves," he said. "We got a donation from one of the bakeries on Granville. Move the soups and cans and make some room for the bread."

"Consider it done. Hey, have you seen Amanda lately?"

"She's gone, kid. Let it go."

My gut dropped. There was too much truth in his words. But I had to fight. "She wouldn't bail—"

Clem's mouth twisted. "Because she's been such a model of stability?"

"Okay, so she's had some issues—"

He snorted. "That girl never met a chemical she didn't like."

If I had lived her life, I would probably have been BFFs with every drug out there too. "Yeah, but things are different now—"

"Because she decided to clean up her life?" asked Clem. "Get a job, get an

5

education? And all thanks to some mysterious *friend*."

"Uh…" I mumbled. There are a lot of rules when you call the streets home. One of the big rules is don't trust everyone. In fact, barely trust anyone. And when you find someone you trust, don't *ever* talk about their business. It wasn't my place to talk about the guy she had met and why she had kept him a secret. And even though I was dying to ask, no way was I going to question Clem on how he knew about all of that.

He pointed to his chest. "Soldier. Decorated veteran. Ran all kinds of missions for the military." He pointed at me. "Rookie."

"I'm the Man," Clem continued, giving me a long pointed look. "I know and see everything." He set the clipboard on the counter and folded his arms. Then gave me a stare that had probably made the opposing armies toss down their guns in surrender. "So how much longer you gonna run around pretending you wear Speedos and not bikinis?"

I was too surprised to blink.

His tone became serious. "You still in the kind of trouble where you got to pretend you're a boy?"

My blush warmed my cheeks, and I was glad my African-Chinese heritage hid it. "Not really. It's just habit, and besides, I figured I'd give you a heart attack if I suddenly showed up as a girl."

"Gotta have a heart for that, kid. Besides, I knew you were a girl the first time I saw you two years ago."

"Please."

"I see you, kid." He gave me a gentle push in the direction of the soup shelves. "I've always seen you. Amanda too. Trust me—she's gone."

His words made my shoulders go stiff. She'd been a friend when I thought I would be alone and lonely forever.

It wasn't like her to disappear without a goodbye. I headed to the shelves, happy for the distraction to collect my emotions.

There was a TV by the boxes of food. I left it on the news station. Clem had a thing for staying up-to-date—even though he swore it was all propaganda and lies. I was ten minutes into filling the shelves with soups and canned vegetables when the reporter's voice caught my attention.

"*Meena Sharma was a decorated Vancouver detective.*"

I stopped, turning to face the screen.

"*She was arrested last month in connection with a house fire two years ago—*"

My heart contracted at the emotionless reporting of the end of my family.

"*—killed in the blaze—*"

Murdered, I silently corrected the perky blond with the helmet hair.

"*—were forty-year-old Emma Ling and her children, Danny, six, and Josephine, fourteen.*"

Danny, who would never learn to ride a bike without training wheels. Mom, who would never see me graduate from high school. And Emily, a foster kid and friend who was mistaken for me. Even though the reporter was technically wrong about whose body was found that night, she was right on the part that mattered. I *had* died that night. Burned to ash along with everything I had ever loved in this world.

"*Sharma remains in critical condition following a prison stabbing—*" The TV clicked off.

I spun around to see Clem right behind me. "Turn it back on! It's important."

He cocked an eyebrow. "Why? What do you care about a corrupt cop?"

My mind scrambled for a plausible answer. "Didn't you say she came in here a few weeks back, looking for Amanda?"

"I saw her *with* Amanda."

"See?" I folded my arms and leaned against the counter. "I could've missed an important clue with the news story. Something that would help me find Amanda."

Clem gave me a look that could shrivel lettuce. But then he shrugged and turned the TV back on. "Watch that heart of yours, kid. It'll be your downfall."

I ignored him, my attention on the news story. But the broadcast had already moved on to some dancing-pig video that had gone viral.

"I don't know what's worse," said Clem. "The lack of real information given in news bites or the fact that the woman can jump from talking about a murdered family to waltzing pork without giving herself whiplash."

"I would know the whole story if you hadn't shut off the TV."

"What's to know? The cop got what was coming to her," said Clem. "Someone stabbed her in the prison washroom. I doubt she'll survive." He strode over to talk to a lanky kid in skinny jeans.

I wished I'd been there when she'd been stabbed. Wished I could've been there when she took her last breath.

While Clem directed the kitchen traffic, I texted Raven the news about Meena. Then I waited for a reply. None came, which probably meant she was with Emmett, the two of them in a tree, *k-i-s-s-i-n-g*. I sighed. Love was such a pain. Come to think of it, so was Raven. A sister from a different mister could still be as annoying as a sister from the same mister.

Of course, thinking about her and Emmett made me think of Jace, and he came with a slew of four-letter words, including *s-t-a-y* and *a-w-a-y*.

"Hey, kid."

I raised my gaze to Clem.

Clem was walking toward me, a bean-pole kid at his side. "Show Ian the ropes."

Living on the streets, you learn to read people fast, and this kid was a screenshot of pain and confusion. When you're homeless, you also learn to keep your mouth shut. I ignored the cuts and bruises on his body, the too-old clothing, the too-pale skin and the dark circles under his eyes.

"Hi, Ian," I said, not trying to shake his hand or anything. I had been working hard at staying healthy and fit. Ian looked like he was a human party venue for the flu bug. "So it's pretty basic. Stock shelves, do what Clem says, and never agree to any of his ideas."

Ian swallowed, and as soon as Clem was out of earshot, he took a gulp of air like he was getting ready to ask me something big.

While he took another breath, I held mine.

"Listen, I need your help."

The tone of his voice signaled trouble. I pretended I hadn't heard him. I had enough problems, and I was in no mood to add more. "Okay, sure, I can help with the stacking. Just watch—"

"No, not this." He stepped closer, and I got a whiff of an unfortunately familiar smell. "Something else."

If he was sleeping in the sewers, as his aroma was suggesting, I knew what kind of help he wanted. I wasn't about to give it. "If you're looking for drugs—"

"No!" He glanced over at Clem and lowered his voice. "Something else... *someone* else."

"We're all looking for someone or something." I hoped he would take the hint and stop talking.

"You don't—"

Man, he looked ready to cry, and I didn't have it in me to break his heart. I sighed. "Okay. You got my attention, but you got to be more specific."

"You lost a friend, right? Me too."

Bing, bing, bing. Now my radar was on high alert. I had been asking around about Amanda, checking the homeless network and vendors on the street. It was possible he had heard about my search. But the concrete jungle has dangerous animals living in it, and I wasn't about to admit to anything until I knew if this kid was prey or predator.

"That it?"

Hope brightened his eyes. "Word is, you're looking for a chick named Amanda."

Give the homeless network credit. They are better than cell towers and Google combined. "Yeah."

"I'm trying to find my friend Dwayne. I haven't seen him in over a month."

I shrugged. "And I can help…how?"

"They disappeared around the same time."

"I don't know what you're talking about."

"Don't play me. I know you've been asking about your friend."

My eyes narrowed. "And how do you know that?"

"Because we all run in the same circles. Because Dwayne was homeless. Amanda was homeless. You start asking questions about a missing kid, people automatically start to talk about other missing kids." He looked a bit amazed at my apparent stupidity.

But I wasn't being stupid. I was double-checking his sources. And seeing if he had anything concrete to offer. Tracking the homeless was a tough job. We were always moving, always looking for a new place to call home. Our need to find that place was what made us such attractive targets for the criminal element. If and when we disappeared, who would know? No one. And who cared when we went missing? Less than no one.

Ian pulled the sleeves of his sweater over his fingers. "I was hoping you had some info on Amanda."

"Sorry, kid. I got nothing. But tell me about Dwayne. Maybe we can track him." I glanced over at Clem and saw him giving me major stinkeye.

He came our way, the slight hitch in his stride the only evidence of his prosthetic leg.

"Stack as we talk." I grabbed some cans, moved the older ones to the front and stuck the newer ones at the back.

Clem paused, then returned to his work.

"Dwayne's had trouble," said Ian.

I snorted. "That's a mandatory requirement for our kind. What made him run in the first place?"

"His dad used him as a punching bag. So Dwayne bailed a couple years back. Got caught up in the usual, looking for love in all the wrong places." The skin on Ian's face tightened. "It got worse when the gangs found him."

So far, Dwayne was sounding a lot like the male version of Amanda.

"But things changed a few months ago. It was like he found religion or something," said Ian. "He started going to Narcotics Anonymous, Alcoholics Anonymous, the works. Signed up for classes for his GED. It was crazy."

"Doesn't sound crazy to me."

"Yeah?" His question held the challenge. "Even when I tell you all this happened because of some guy he met? Just like how all of it happened for Amanda because of some guy she met?"

"Still doesn't sound crazy." Creepy was more like it. Amanda and Dwayne were paper copies of each other—both attracted to the wrong crowd. And if someone was collecting street kids like them, it meant more were in danger of disappearing.

Ian was going to get himself killed if he started asking too many questions. It was up to me to warn him off. "Sounds exactly like what Amanda did too." I shrugged and hoped it looked casual. "Could be some nonprofit or church guy. You know those religious types. Always trying to feed us and make our lives better. Maybe Amanda and Dwayne went with them."

"And x'd us out of their lives?"

Another shrug. "Maybe the guy told them we were like a drug addiction—you know, hanging out with other homeless. Break the cycle, find new friends, obey curfew, eat your veggies. That kind of thing."

"Did she get all secretive on you too? 'Cause Dwayne did, and being secretive isn't the way the religious types are."

My stocking of the shelves slowed as I considered his question. "Yeah, she did. She'd take off, go to these…meetings." I felt bad for icing him out. He had been a stand-up guy when it came to giving out info. I could return the favor, even if it was a nothing bit of info. "She promised she wasn't meeting any more 'boyfriends,' but—"

"Just like Dwayne." Ian sighed.

"When was the last time you saw him?"

"He said he had to go to an appointment, never came back."

Just like Amanda. "Do you have any idea where he went? General area?"

He shook his head. Clearly, he didn't have any information that would help me find Amanda. Another dead end. "Sorry, I can't help you," I said.

"But..." He came in close, whispering. "I heard about you...and your team."

My eyebrows shot up. "My *what*?"

"Your team. You, a climber chick, a hacker and a boxer."

Oh boy. There were a million things wrong with this. It was one thing for us to know we were a team and doing stuff that could get us arrested, maimed or killed. But the bigger problem was that we'd obviously been visible enough when we took down our bad guys that we were now making waves. Which meant we could be tracked.

"You took down some heavy-duty bad guys, right?" Ian asked after it was clear I wasn't going to answer him.

I respected the homeless network, but I couldn't trust its discretion. In this world, trust could get you killed. "Maybe. Maybe not," I replied. "Can't say I know what you're talking about."

"If you did it once, you can do it again." He stood a little straighter, his tone changing from pleading to commanding. "You can't let Amanda and Dwayne fall."

"I don't have a passport," I shot back, "so take someone else on your guilt trip. If I *could* help, I would." Actually, I had an idea brewing, but I didn't know if it would work. No point getting his hopes up.

I went to the counter and grabbed one of Clem's business cards. "Take this. Clem's a good guy. If you find anything out and I'm not around, let him know. He'll pass it on."

Ian crumpled the card, shoving it into his pocket. "Thanks for nothing," he mumbled, then stomped away.

His gruff words hurt. Not that I showed it. One day he'd learn the rule that "ya gotta be cruel to be kind." He was mad I wasn't jumping in to help him, but I wasn't going to do anything to risk his safety. I could do all the heavy lifting, sifting and asking questions on my own. I finished stocking the shelves, then went to Clem to collect my "payment"—a sack of groceries to last the week.

"I put something special in there for you," Clem said, handing me the bag.

"That's terrifying."

"Soldier up, kid. It's a Wagon Wheel. With your mouth, I figure you could use some sweetness."

"Talk like that and I'll never leave," I said.

"That's terrifying." He gave an exaggerated shudder to prove his point.

I jerked my head in Ian's direction. "Look out for him. His friend's gone missing the same way Amanda did."

"First thing you learn in the military is to spread your resources where they matter. Those kids are gone. To heaven or hell, I don't know. But you're better off spending your time focused on other things."

Maybe, but I also knew the soldier's creed: never leave a man behind.

TWO

I did have one strong hope for finding Amanda, and I put it into effect the next day. Bentley. That guy could hack the Pentagon in thirty seconds if he wanted. School was out so I figured I'd find him at his usual hangout—Tron's grocery store on East Georgia.

I did a quick detour to my trailer for a change of clothes and gender. After two years of living on the streets and pretending to be a boy, getting in touch with my inner girl was taking some getting used to—but I was up for anything that didn't involve baggy jeans.

I headed to Tron's and found Bentley at the ATM machine, probably hacking the system and taking money from his father's account. Considering the hell Daddy Dearest had put him through, including numerous excruciating surgeries to "fix" his dwarfism, I didn't blame him.

I'd helped Bentley and his brother, Jace, deal with their dad. And it hadn't been easy. Jace had been tortured and Raven and I had almost been arrested, but the guys had found their retribution.

I stepped close and said his name.

When Bentley didn't answer, I touched his shoulder.

He jumped a bit, then spun toward me, pulling a bud from his ear. Techno music, made tinny by the small speakers, pumped with its repetitive beat.

"I got a job for you," I said.

"What, not even a *hello, how are you, Bentley*?"

"I got—"

"I heard you the first time." He dumped his buds in the messenger bag at his feet. They fell in between the giant bags of candy and chocolate stuffed inside. "What's the job?"

"Track a phone for me."

Bentley rolled his eyes and hefted the bag over his shoulder. "I thought it was going to be something hard. This is play-school crap."

"If I wanted to give you an impossible task, I would ask you to try to find your brother's heart."

He didn't bother to hide his smile. "Let's go to the park."

I followed him out, giving the store a quick once-over for security. Tron had been good to me. Once in a while I'd test his surveillance system by shoplifting something, and then I would bring the stuff back to him. In return, he'd give me groceries. Regular kids may live for their allowance, but on the streets you'd die for food. Part of me wanted to see him one last time, to thank him for his kindness. Most of me knew it would be stupid and dangerous. Let him think the "boy" he helped had died or moved on.

Bentley and I stepped into the overcast Vancouver day, then moved to a secluded bench in the park. I gave him Amanda's cell number and waited for Bentley to work his magic.

"Here." He spun the laptop to face me. "The last ping was on North Lagoon Drive and Tatlow Walk."

"Stanley Park? What was she doing there?" I leaned in. "Can you get something more specific?"

"Wouldn't matter. The phone hasn't been used in weeks."

My insides went cold. She hadn't texted me in a while, but I'd told myself there were a lot of reasons for that. Like, maybe she was sliding back into her previous life and was too ashamed to talk to me.

But Amanda was a freak about that phone. She was always texting or doing online searches or watching puppy videos. If her cell hadn't been used at all, that could only mean big, bad things for my friend. I stood. "Okay. Thanks."

Bentley flipped the computer closed. "You want some help? Jace—" He stopped talking as a black SUV pulled to the curb. "He's here."

The tinted window rolled down and revealed Bentley's older brother. His expression was lost behind his sunglasses, but I got the distinct impression he was giving me a once-over. In a boy-likes-girl kind of way. I ignored that feeling. Just like I ignored the urge to check him out in a girl-likes-boy kind of way. Feelings weren't anything but chemicals I reminded myself. I wasn't about to get addicted to his drug, no matter how amazing he looked or how devoted he was to his brother.

I had enough trouble dealing with my feelings for Raven and Bentley. The more you cared for someone, the more hurt you could get. Not just by them, but by those who would use them to get to you. I didn't need to add Jace to my already complicated life.

"He'll help," said Bentley. "Tell him your problem."

Jace smirked. "Yeah, tell me your secrets and I'll solve everything."

And there went the fuzzy boy-girl feelings. "I'm good," I said. "I don't need anything from you." I took a breath and smiled at Bentley. "You, on the other hand, I owe. Thanks for helping with the phone."

Bentley shrugged. "Whatever."

"Have fun, boys." I headed away from them, resisting the urge to look over my shoulder. A few seconds later a blur of black metal broke into my peripheral vision. The suv swooped from the road to the pavement and blocked my path. "Gimme a break," I said as Jace rose out of the driver's seat. "Just because your family owns most of Vancouver doesn't give you the right to drive like a jerk."

"Raven texted. Said she needs us at the houseboat."

"Raven needs a lot of things. Therapy comes to mind." I stepped around him, but Jace grabbed my hand.

I pulled out of his grasp. "Raven's a big girl. She can take care of herself."

"She says it's important. Code Red."

I groaned. About a month back, we had become a team because each of us had a bad guy to bring down.

High on success, we'd promised to always look out for each other. Code Red. I couldn't ignore it.

I trudged to the suv. "First thing we're talking about is changing our signal. *Code Red* is totally cliché."

Jace grinned. "Raven may be in serious trouble, and your priority is the words we use?"

"The last time Raven was in trouble, it involved car thefts, a dead kid and scaling the walls of buildings. Concentrating on terminology seems the safest thing to do."

That made him laugh. "We'll stop off at the army-supply store. Pick you up some Kevlar."

I opened the door of the vehicle and was blasted by a wave of techno music. "Toss in some earplugs, and we've got a deal."

THREE

The door swung open and Raven gaped at
us. "Did I miss the invite to the reunion
party?"

Okay, that was a weird way to say
hello, especially since she was the one
who had texted for help. But before I
could ask what her problem was, Bentley
pushed past. We followed him into the
houseboat.

I took in the candles and the heady
scent of garlic and onions in the air. And
Raven. Her dark hair long and loose, a
fire-red halter top and skinny jeans that
hugged in all the right places. "Oh boy.

If there's an emergency, you called the wrong people, *girlita*. I think you were looking for the loooooove doctor—ow!" I rubbed the spot where she punched me.

"Seriously, what are you newbs doing here? And talk fast."

"Got a text you were in dire straits." Jace headed to a pot of spaghetti sauce bubbling away on the propane stove. He helped himself to a chunk of garlic bread on the counter and dipped it in. "Needs more basil," he declared.

"There's no emergency." Raven glared at him. "But keep dissing my cooking, and we'll have to call the paramedics."

Jace helped himself to another piece of bread. "If you didn't text the Code Red, who did?"

I knew. Spinning, I fixed my eyes on Bentley. "You hacked her phone. What's going on?"

"Kids are contacting me and asking for our help. They're in serious trouble. The kind of trouble where adults can't—

or won't—help. A lot of times, the adult in their life *is* the trouble. These kids need help, and we can give it. We have the money, the skills. Raven, you can climb any building and pick any lock. Jo, you've got your mad art skills and can blend in anywhere. I have the tech skills, and Jace—"

"If you say he's the brains of the operation, I'm walking," Raven said.

"If you say he's the brains," I said, "I'm asking for a CT scan, an X-ray and an MRI, 'cause I'm not buying it." I cocked my head and smiled at Jace. "Although I would argue he's got such a thick skull we could use it as a battering ram, and he is the perfect height for reaching stuff on the top shelf."

Jace glowered.

Bentley ignored me and kept talking. "Plus, Jace and I have the money and the clubhouse and the stuff. We've got the goods to help any kid. We need to do more than just sit around"—his gaze moved to the stove—"making spaghetti sauce."

His Robin Hood speech got groans from all of us.

"For the record," said Raven, "marinara is a lot harder to make than you think." No one commented.

"What happened over the past few weeks was great, but we have to cool things down," I said to Bentley. "Word is spreading, and that's going to get us on the authorities' radar. We can't risk it."

"Then why are we here?" Bentley made eye contact with each of us. "If we hadn't joined forces and worked together, at least two of us would be dead." He held up his phone. "It's life-and-death for them too. You going to tell me our lives are worth more than theirs?"

That got me. I sighed. Holding out my hand, I said, "Gimme."

"A kid's friend is missing," Bentley said as he gave me his cell.

I scrolled through the texts. "You guys are off the hook. This kid already contacted me. I think his friend is linked to Amanda." I tossed the phone back to Bentley. "I've got this."

"You might need our help. Some real help, not just play-school stuff like when you had me ping the cell today," said Bentley. "I may not look like much, but I have brains and a heart, and I can make the world a better place."

Crap. This kid could make me go soggier than a tissue left in a rainstorm. "This is street business," I told him. "It's dangerous—"

I held up my hand as he opened his mouth to protest. "I'm not arguing your heart, your skills or your brain. I am saying that you live in a five-thousand-square-foot mansion, and that's just one of your many, many houses. You can do a lot of things, Bentley, but street fighting isn't one of them."

I had to get out of there. "Have a nice dinner," I said as I headed for the door.

Raven stopped me. "You sure you want to ice us out?" she asked, her voice low.

I glanced at the guys. Bentley, head bent, jaw hard. Jace, protective as he leaned into his brother's ear and quietly talked.

"Come on, Raven. The streets would eat these guys alive. Jace, maybe he'd get out with a broken jaw and ribs. But you know what would happen to Bentley. You know what the scum element will do to anyone who's different."

She cast a worried eye over our friends.

"The streets are just roads they drive down," I said, "but for you and me, they're the roof and walls we call home. We know how to stay safe. They don't."

"Fine, but I can help—"

"And risk whatever's left of the car-theft gang coming after you? Forget it."

"Jo—"

"How about this? Let me do the first round, okay? I'll call you in if I get in over my head." I squeezed her hand. Smiled big. Then, to make sure she didn't pick up on the fact I hadn't *promised* to call, I said, "Water Charlie. That weed looks like it needs water."

"It's a begonia, and you know it."

"Weed." I stepped through the door before she could think too hard on what I had said.

"Flower!" Her voice followed me into the darkening night.

I wanted to get to Amanda's last known location, the spot her cell had placed her. It was a stupid waste of time. I knew she wouldn't be there, knew I wouldn't find any evidence of her.

Amanda was a creature of habit. I had never known her to hang out on Lagoon Drive. Still, I wanted to go stand on the same spot and see if I could figure out what had made her go there.

Odds were, it was probably that guy. The one she had fallen in love with. Just like she fell in love with any guy who smiled her way. But I didn't have much to go on. She'd told me he was someone who had lived on the streets but had managed to get off them. And he was going to help her do the same thing. Thanks to her so-called savior, she had enrolled in night school and had talked about moving into a halfway house. But now she was gone, capital-G gone. And I was sure her boyfriend was behind her disappearance.

The question was, was she gone because he had pushed her back into her old prostituting ways, or had something else happened? I didn't know, and either possibility filled me with dread.

FOUR

Before I started scouting for Amanda again, there was something else I had to do. I had to help out the other folks who relied on me. Some homeless people didn't mind soup kitchens or coming in from the cold and bunking in a shelter. But some were too old, too scared, too starved of hope to move from the cold corners and dark alleys they called home. I headed to the streets and handed out boxes and cans of food from the bag of groceries Clem had given me. The Wagon Wheel I kept for myself. Clem and I weren't into declarations of friendship and affection, but I knew what the treat meant.

After I'd given out the last can and gotten a grateful smile in return, I turned my attention to my missing friend. No surprise, I had no luck. If there had been any trace of Amanda, the rain, sand and visitors to the water had erased all of it.

I headed back to the community kitchen. Figured I'd let Clem know he'd been right—he'd love that. I also figured I could use his military background. Maybe he'd see something in the circumstances of Amanda's disappearance that I'd missed. When I got there, he was on the phone. He pivoted, looked at me, then gave me a *come here* wave.

"Yeah," he said to the person on the phone. "I'll be there." He ended the call, then shoved his cell in his back pocket. "You're with me."

"Where are we going?"

"Morgue."

"Disco's dead and they need you to identify the corpse?"

"Your snark would be a lot more believable if your voice didn't catch."

"That's not emotion," I said as I followed him out the door. "That's a reaction to your cologne."

"Maybe I should leave you here."

I put my hands up in a surrender gesture. "I'm raising the white flag." If I wanted to tag along, I'd better let him have this round. "Sorry, boss."

Clem's suv chirped as he unlocked the doors. I climbed into the passenger seat. "So tell me again, why are we going to the morgue?"

"They found a body with my business card on it." He started the car and pulled out of the lot.

My breath escaped in a fast *whoosh*. "I gave Ian your card yesterday."

"Yeah." His voice was grim. "And the body's male." He glanced over at me briefly and then went back to watching the road. "There's something else."

I braced myself.

"The coroner said they've got a few Jane and John Does, bodies that haven't been claimed. He figures they're homeless. Thought we could help identify some."

"Yeah." I kept my voice steady. "No problem."

"You sure you're up to this, kid? Prepared for what you might find?"

I nodded. Ever since I'd succeeded in finding justice for my family, the days had seemed brighter, the world more hopeful. Not anymore. The sun was setting, and the world was growing cold.

We drove the rest of the way in silence. Parked in silence. Filled out the paperwork in silence. Went to the quiet room with the curtained window and the smell of disinfectant.

The coroner came into the room, introduced herself and explained that she would have her assistant pull back the curtains. We'd see the body, identify it.

That's when I spoke up. "I'm not identifying anyone from here. I want in there."

The coroner's gaze flicked to Clem, then came back to me. "It's not policy—"

"I don't care what your policy is." I strode toward her. "You said there's a bunch of Jane and John Does, right?" Before she could answer, I continued my rant. "They're homeless. Invisible. Untouched. Unloved. Barely acknowledged in life. They deserve more in death." The coroner still wasn't sure. I flashed her a withering smile and said, "If you're worried my mommy and daddy might be upset, let me make it easy for you. I don't have either." I walked toward the door that separated the viewing room from where the bodies would be wheeled in.

She turned to Clem, clearly hoping he would step in.

"He can't help," I said. "The man's ancient—and he was in the war. He's so old, he was probably in all of them. Most days he can't remember to put on his pants. You want to trust an ID to him?"

Clem glared at me. "I don't know what you're talking about."

"You see what I mean? We gonna do this, or you just want to validate my parking?" I straightened my back and glared at her.

The coroner sighed and knocked on the window.

A young guy came into view.

The coroner pointed at the door, then pointed again when he looked puzzled.

The guy shrugged, then walked over and unlocked the door.

I didn't look at Clem as I walked inside. Didn't think about why death had seen fit to visit me—again—to take someone I knew and leave me behind. Didn't think about the truth of why I wanted to be in the room: that I had to touch them, to make sure the bodies were real and not some twisted trick or prank.

I stared at the white sheet in front of me. Cataloged the dips and peaks as it draped over the body. Concentrated on lines and color, turned it all into an art exercise so I wouldn't have to think about the lost kid lying underneath. The forgotten one who would never find home.

I stepped out of the way as the assistant coroner moved in. His long brown fingers gripped the white sheet, and he pulled it back with a grace and gentleness that hit me hard.

The punch to the gut became a one-two blow when I saw Ian's lifeless face.

I forgot about the smell of disinfectant and formaldehyde, the squeak of the coroner's sneakers, the shriek of the thoughts in my head. Only one thing filled my vision and my awareness: Ian needed justice, and I was going to get it for him.

FIVE

Ian's face was barely a face anymore. Someone had beaten him to a pulp. I moved closer to him. Reached out my hand and touched his cold forehead. "Where was he found?" I asked.

"Across the water on Mitchell Island," replied the lady coroner.

Bentley had said Amanda's phone had last pinged at North Lagoon Drive and Tatlow Walk. But Ian's body had been found at the opposite end of the city. That meant either her disappearance wasn't connected to Ian's or the two *were* connected and someone was trying real hard to hide the fact.

"Cause of death?" asked Clem.

"Massive internal bleeding," said the coroner.

I appreciated that she wasn't using a bunch of medical jargon. "How long did it take for him—"

"Not long," she said softly.

Let the answer stay at that, I thought. Don't torture yourself with how many minutes it would have taken for him to die. Don't ask if he was conscious to the last moment.

"What else can you tell us?" asked Clem.

"I shouldn't—" She shifted backward. "There's a police investigation—"

"Right." I couldn't keep the sarcasm out of my voice. "And homeless deaths are such a high priority. Wouldn't want to risk messing with a high conviction rate or anything."

"Easy, kid," said Clem. "She didn't do this to Ian."

"Ian. That was his name?" Coroner Guy held up a clipboard.

I nodded, my anger starting to subside. "Yeah. I didn't catch his last name."

"Nothing else?" He sounded disappointed. "Nothing about his home life?"

"He was a homeless kid," I said. "We all have the same story—violence, neglect and abuse. What else is there to know?"

"Sorry," he mumbled. "Just thought you might have more for us to go on."

"Can't you run his prints? Maybe he was in the system—" I saw the look that passed between the doctors. "What?"

"Whoever did this—" the lady coroner's mouth moved, but no sound came out as she considered her words "—made sure there were no prints left behind."

My mind ran straight to all the ways this could have been done. "Before or after he died?"

"Postmortem. After he died," she said.

"Small mercy," murmured Clem.

Too small. "You said there was a police investigation?" I was like a dog with a bone. A growly, hungry dog with a too-small bone.

"He's not the first body to be brought in like this," said Coroner Guy. "We figure—" He stopped and bent his head over the clipboard.

"Logic says you take off fingers to prevent identification," I said. "But whoever did this didn't go through Ian's pockets, or else he would have taken Clem's business card. Which means whoever did this just did it for kicks."

The lady coroner's face went white. "I'm sorry," she said gently, "that his last minutes were with someone who had such little regard for him."

"Me too," I told her. "How many have there been?"

"Eight. Five boys, three girls. The girls weren't beaten to death, but they had been beaten in the recent past. ODs, the lot of them. But all the bodies have defensive wounds, old bruises and burns." The coroners both frowned. "The weird thing is what we found in their stomachs. These kids were eating better than most North Americans. Plus, tox screens indicate they were taking high-quality vitamins and supplements. It doesn't make sense."

Maybe not to her, but I knew what had ended these kids. And proving it was not going to be easy. Bentley was about to get his wish. I needed his brain to help me navigate the hidden underbelly of the Darknet.

SIX

"You're quiet tonight." Raven jumped from the bottom rung of the building's fire escape ladder, and landed beside me.

"Thought you liked the strong, silent type," I shot back.

"No, *hermana*," said Raven. "That's your brand."

"I don't know what's more disturbing," I said. "Your hacking the Spanish language or that you're calling me 'sister.'"

"Sarcasm, I assure you."

I put my hand to my heart and gave her a wounded look. "I know, and that's what hurts most."

She snorted and punched me on the arm.

"Come on, let's grab a drink."

"I get the whole coming out from under the sewers is big-time awesome for you," Raven said, "but do we have to hit every coffee shop in the downtown core?"

"I did two years of eating from garbage cans—"

"And now you have a chance to eat something more than day-old bread."

I faced her. "The words are right. But my voice isn't that high or breathy."

"It is when Jace's around—"

"Shut it."

We grabbed a couple of smoothies and croissants from one of the shops on Robson—my treat—then went our separate ways.

I headed home. Raven may have razzed me about my living it up after my days on the street but my current life wasn't perfect. Sure, I had a new identity. Plus, with the haircut and the weight

I'd gained, I didn't look like a coatrack anymore. But I wasn't stupid. It was still dangerous out in the open and living in the real world still meant hiding from most people.

Most people didn't include Vincent. He had known me before my family died and he had been the one who'd recognized my talent. Thanks to him, I had learned how to forge masters like Leonardo da Vinci and Francisco Goya. And double thanks to Vincent, I had used that talent to make a little cash.

Now that I had found justice for my family, it was time to get off the streets. I used my art funds to get some clothes, food, and a comfortable place to sleep. Home was a cushy doublewide trailer that sat in a park full of Vincent's old ex-con buddies. Men and women who'd had enough of the life and had no desire to be tracked by the authorities. One of the forgers who had struck it rich by doing a Monet better than the master himself had also been smart enough to get out before she got caught.

She'd set up a series of dummy corporations, and ran all the park's bills through them. I paid my share for the electricity, water, and heat, but there was no record of my name or my existence. And I'd made sure to set up my bank funds via the Swiss. Those guys were good for more than just chocolate and cuckoo clocks.

And that cash was going to come in handy. Before I could get Bentley's help, I needed to get some bitcoin, the currency of choice for the Darknet. But the Darknet was a warped network, full of crazies and psychos, and they were all paranoid. I wanted to give him as much cover as I could.

After I showered, I played it safe. Went for a boy disguise: long black jacket, short black wig, make-up to darken my skin, and a light covering of facial hair.

Jace didn't know it, but Bentley had lent me one of their family cars. I'd asked him for something low-key. Apparently in that family, low-key was a silver Porsche Spyder.

I headed back into town. The seller of the bitcoins wanted to meet at the waterfront near Bella Gelateria, an ice-cream parlor. I left the car in a public parking lot, then made my way to the location.

In the email, the seller had said they'd be wearing a red jacket. I got to the location, expecting some twenty- or thirty-something guy with a scraggly beard, death metal T-shirt, and a chronic case of bad breath. Instead, I found a country club senior citizen standing by the open hood of her Mercedes, the scent of her über-expensive perfume reaching me before I even got close. I hesitated, figuring it must be a coincidence.

"Don't be a moron," she said. "Get over here and let's make the exchange."

Surprise kept my feet glued to the ground.

She gave me an amused smile. "You think you punks invented the outlaw society? I was breaking laws before your mother was even born."

"You're here to sell me digital money," I said, making my way over to her. "Digital. You could have transferred it electronically."

She snorted. "You idiots are exactly why the crime rates are dropping. No sense of showmanship. There was a time when these things were about the experience, the contact…"

I opted not to get into a fight with a crazy seventy-year-old who thought she was a gangster. "Whatever." I dug in my pocket and pulled out the money.

The old bat gave me the information for the digital transfer of the bitcoins, dropped the hood of her car, wished me a nice day and took off. I texted Bentley and let him know I had what he needed.

He phoned and told me to wait for the next move. I headed to the ice-cream parlor and got a double scoop. Snagging a spot on a rusting bike rack that had seen better days, I bit into the sugary snack and took a moment to enjoy the feel of the sun on my skin, the wind in my hair. I hadn't even eaten half of the cone when I got the text alert.

Shielding the screen from the sun, I scanned the message and smiled. That kid was something else. Not just fast, but careful. To anyone else who saw the text, it would look like someone had left their phone unlocked, stuck it in their back pocket, sat down and accidently activated the keyboard. The message was a random set of numbers and letters. But Bentley was a hacker genius. He'd designed one algorithm that put his info into code and another that translated the message.

I opened the app, translated the information and got what I needed. The location of the next fight. Then, as always, I deleted the texts. My ice cream was melting, and so was my latest lead.

I scarfed the rest of the cone and made my way back to the car. Time to get back to work. Top down, catching air and rubber, I headed for the nearest lonely alley with no cameras.

After tucking the car behind a set of garbage bins, I got rid of the dude get-up. I stowed the clothes in the back of the car. After another ten minutes to stash the vehicle in another public lot, I headed to the subway. Bentley had done his part. Now it was up to me. First rule of any fight: know your opponent. Time to hit the streets and find out who was the head guy behind the club. It was all happy-scrappy to know where the fight was, but if I couldn't get the head guy, it was a waste of time. He would just reorganize. More kids would go missing or die. No way was I going to let anyone else plunge into the darkness that had consumed Amanda and Ian.

SEVEN

People always tell you who they are in the things they say and the things they don't say. Instinct told me that Coroner Guy had been raised middle class, hadn't ever been a rebel and had respectable friends. And he was new enough to his job that he hadn't yet seen the dark side of humanity.

His theory was that the kids had gotten into some street beefs with other kids and had tried to fight off their attacker. He wasn't all wrong. They'd fought, all right, but it wasn't an attacker. It was an opponent. Those kids had been part of an illegal fighting ring. They'd been beaten

NATASHA DEEN

and then beaten again over the course of a few weeks. If they had really died after one fight, there wouldn't have been fading bruises. And the reason the girls didn't have any fresh injuries was probably because the gang had them working the guys in the crowd. Flip their hair, flirt. Nothing like a bunch of hot girls to add atmosphere and sizzle and get spectators to open their wallets and bet.

How was I so sure? I knew all about the fight club. Every street kid did, but not because we talked about it. We feared it. Stayed silent about it. Just like scientists can detect black holes because of their effect on the matter around them, street kids recognize the shadow the club casts on all of us.

Kids showing up at the shelters with bruises and cuts they wouldn't talk about.

Kids showing up at the shelters with wads of cash spattered with blood.

Kids not showing up at the shelters.

Kids disappearing altogether.

If a kid found an adoptive home or went back home, word spread. The hope burned bright and clean and kept us warm while we slept in our cardboard boxes. But kids lost to the club? They became the ultimate black hole. No light. No air. And you didn't ask questions, because asking questions sucked you into a place that would crush you.

Ian had died because of the fight club. And if he had been there, chances were Amanda was there too. Anyone with half a brain would have walked away. Fight club was the only place rival gangs seemed to get along. If "getting along" could ever describe the way they behaved with each other. But they had a system, and it had worked for a long time.

Each gang brought a roster of fighters.

Each gang brought a crowd of spectators.

One gang hosted—provided a venue, protection for the organizers and security for the audience.

Then it was all about collecting the bets and forcing kids to bash each other's heads in. The host gang collected the winnings, took a cut, distributed the cash.

The next time there was a fight, another gang would play host by providing a location and protection.

There were all kinds of side businesses to the fights—drugs, money laundering—but it worked for the gangs, kept the police off their trail and provided entertainment for people who'd lost their souls a long time ago.

Logic, common sense and survival told me to run. To listen to Clem, bid *sayonara* to Amanda, light a candle for Ian and Dwayne and get on with my life. But I wouldn't have had a life without Amanda, and I couldn't—wouldn't—let her fall.

I took the subway to the Stadium-Chinatown station. Then I spent too many hours walking around Gastown, strolling the tree-lined streets, searching for any of my kin—fellow homeless—

to get information. Clean stucco and brick buildings gave way to trash, iron-barred windows and the smell of despair as I headed east to Nanaimo Street. The clientele on the pavement changed too. From middle and upper class, well dressed and well fed, to those who used the ether of alcohol to pretend they wore more than rags, and the burn of meth to quiet the ache in their bellies.

Some people might have been scared by the rotting smiles and grizzled hair, but I'd lived on the streets. I knew the inner workings of this jungle the way most people knew the creaks and groans of their homes. I pounded a relentless rhythm on the pavement, checking the doorways and alleys, tapping into every source and contact I knew.

They smiled when they saw me, didn't mind when I got up close and personal and climbed into their boxes with them. But their goodwill vanished when I asked about the club, the gangs and the leader. Some turned back to the bottle in their hand. Most turned from me. A few warned me away. Under a setting sun I took my questions to the other side of the street and, working my way back, got the same answers.

Sort of.

I still didn't have a name for the head guy, but I had a description. He had a gym body without being overly muscled, fair skin, a deep voice and a commanding attitude. It wasn't much, but at least I knew I wasn't looking for an old man with a gut.

By the time I returned to the Porsche, my head hurt, my feet ached, and my brain was focused on one idea. Thanks to the crazy old lady, bitcoins, the Darknet and Bentley's genius, I knew the location of the next fight. My idea? Head to the fight and see if I could pick out the head honcho.

It wouldn't be that hard. Power is like a high-watt lightbulb. The guy's underlings would flock to it like moths. Find the man everyone's trying hard to please, you find the leader behind the club.

Of course, if I was a good girl, I would pass the information on to the cops and let them do their thing. Lucky for me, I'm not a good girl. Besides, the cops aren't my friends.

I stopped in at a brightly lit chain restaurant to get some food. No point wading into hell on an empty stomach. I ordered a loaded burger, fries and a drink. Took my time eating it, both to give myself a break and to give myself time to think. By the time dessert arrived, I knew what I needed to do.

I called Bentley and told him my plan.

He was not happy, but there was no arguing with me.

"Jace isn't around, is he?" I asked.

"No."

"Good. Then I need you to grab some of his clothes. I have to look the part—like a rich guy with nothing better to do. I'll bring his stuff back as soon as I'm done."

"This is a bad idea," said Bentley. "I don't think you should do it alone."

"I won't be alone. You'll be with me via the earpiece you're going to lend me."

That got two seconds of silence. "It's still dangerous. I can't do anything if you're miles away and under attack."

"You couldn't do anything if you were right beside me," I said softly. "These guys carry more than money and keys in their jeans. They're going to have guns and knives."

"I'm sorry—is that supposed to make me *want* to help you or agree to let you go in there?"

"What if I said pretty please and took you out for ice cream?" I asked.

Ignoring me, he said, "Jace's clothes will be too big. Way too long and too wide."

"I can make it work. Trust me."

He sighed. "You're going to do it anyway, aren't you? It won't matter whether I help or not."

"Yeah," I said, "but I'd love your help. Dynamic duo and all that."

Bentley was silent.

"Come on, Bentley-Bear," I said. "I can't do it without you."

"Fine." He sighed. "But nix that nickname. I don't think it suits me."

"Bentley-Boo?"

He hung up.

I left the waitress a 20 percent tip for not mentioning the layer of street perfume I'd brought back with me. Then I was back in the car on my way to Bentley's house, the moonlight getting brighter. Too soon, given how much I was enjoying the sound of rubber on asphalt, I pulled the vehicle into the driveway and approached the massive glass-and-wrought-iron double doors that served as the front entrance of the house.

Bentley opened the door before I could ring the bell. "We've got a problem," he said.

"The clothes?"

Before he could answer, the door opened all the way. Jace. He looked tired, haunted, but now wasn't the time to worry about him.

"No, not the clothes," Jace said. "Your problem is with me."

"Thanks, Sherlock, but I already made that deduction a long time ago." I pushed past the guys and stepped into the marble entryway. Turning to them, I said, "Just how are you looking to be yet another pain in my—"

"You're going to an underground fight club," said Jace.

"You told him?" I turned an accusing glare to Bentley.

The hacker blushed. "I didn't think he'd pull a hissy fit."

"Of course he would. When he's not brooding or wandering the streets, he's channeling his inner diva. How did it not occur to you that he'd pull a hissy fit?"

"*He*"—Jace spoke slowly—"is right here."

I ignored him and kept talking to Bentley. "He's like a combination of mother bear and headless chicken—"

"Hey!" Jace lifted his hands in a *what the hell?* gesture.

"I know," said Bentley, "but I thought things had changed."

"With him?" I asked, jerking my thumb in Jace's direction.

"Him is still here and getting more pissed off by the minute," said Jace.

"See?" I said. "Brooding diva."

The muscles of Jace's jaw rippled. "I. Am. Right. Here."

"I know," I said, "but we're trying not to let that ruin our evening."

"This plan won't work." Jace spoke like it was the end of the conversation.

"Of course it will!" I said.

Jace gave me a long look.

"I'm great at makeup and disguise, and Bentley's a superhero with technology.

Trust me, this will work. All I have to do is get in there. Bentley's lending me glasses with a built-in camera and an earpiece. I can document everything, get out and pass the information to Raven. Her boyfriend's the son of a cop. He'll make sure the evidence gets into the right hands."

Jace kept staring.

"Usually I'm all for the silent glares, but I've got to get going. Either use your words or go brood somewhere else."

"Don't try to fool me," he said. "You're not going there to help those kids. You're going there to find Amanda. The kids are just an added bonus."

Seriously. Why was he ragging on me? "So?"

"So you're going to do something stupid," he said. "You'll see her, your emotions will take over, and you'll go all Hulk meets the Punisher."

"My emotions will take over?" Forget the fight club happening later—there was about to be a fight right now. And

I was going to win. "Why? Because I'm a girl?"

He gave me a soft smile. "No, Jo, because we're alike. You told me once that Amanda was the one you watched over, just like I watch over Bentley. I would lose my mind if I saw him in pain and thought I could help."

Crap. Those words were a perfect combo for a TKO on my anger. "I can't argue that. For the record"—I glanced over at Bentley—"if anyone ever hurt you, I would definitely lose my mind."

Bentley rolled his eyes. "You both already proved that, okay? I'm going all squishy with the frickin' touchy-feely emotions, but we've got a job to do." He took a deep breath and let it out. "My brother's right. This is too dangerous for you to do alone."

I opened my mouth to argue, but he was still talking.

"And Jace, Jo is right," he continued. "She has to go in there."

Again, the muscles of Jace's jaw rippled.

"I know how to solve this," Bentley continued. "Go together."

"Great idea," said Jace.

"Bad idea." I shook my head. "Very, very bad idea." I had enough to worry about with my own safety. Now I was supposed to look after a trust-fund kid?

"Bentley, I'll see you around 2 AM," said Jace. "Maybe later. If I'm not back by four, pull up the tracker."

"Whoa, whoa, whoa." I held up my hands. "Who said you were going with me? I didn't agree to that."

"No," Jace said, "but you agreed to let Bentley help. And we both know how smart he is. So if it's an idea he came up with, it must be a good one." He gave me a victorious look.

Crap. He had me.

Jace strode to the curved staircase and grabbed his leather jacket off the banister. "I'll be the voice of reason."

We stared at each other.

"Yeah," Jace said with a smile. "That's freaky for me too."

"You'll stay in the car?" I asked.

"Nice try. I'll be right beside you."

"Making sure I don't do anything stupid," I said.

"It's a big job," he said, "but, luckily, I had lots of protein today."

I surrendered. "Okay."

He gave me a critical look. "That's what you're wearing?"

I looked down at my dark jeggings, black shirt and boots. "What's wrong with it?"

"To this kind of place? You're not dressed up enough," he said. "Bentley, grab something from Mother's closet."

"I'm not wearing fur," I called after Bentley as he headed up the stairs.

"You won't have to," said Jace. "That's for the girls in the inner circle."

Since when did he know so much about illegal fights? I didn't bother to argue.

Jace looked down at me. "But if you feel the need to drape the carcass of a dead animal around your shoulders—"

"You'll volunteer your hide?" I asked.

"Ouch." He put his hand to his heart. "And I was going to take you for some ice cream before we went on our date."

Great. A long car ride with Jace the Sarcastic. This night just couldn't get any better.

EIGHT

The fight was an hour's drive away. No abandoned warehouse this time. We were headed into the woods.

"You okay?" I asked Jace.

"That's a big question."

"You seem unusually quiet, even for you."

Jace smiled, but there was no joy in it. "Why wouldn't I be okay? I've got everything—cars, houses, clothes...kids would kill to be me."

I knew better than to push for information, so I settled back and waited.

After a minute, Jace continued. "What would you do if you found out something about yourself? Something that could destroy everything and everyone around you?"

I reached over and squeezed his hand. "Buddy, we're here for you. It's okay to admit you like boy bands."

He laughed. "Jo, I'm being serious."

"How much destruction's involved?" I let go of his fingers.

"It could hurt Bentley," he said, and I heard the pain in his voice. "Really hurt him."

"Does he deserve to know the truth?" I asked.

"Yes, but it's more than just my family and the team. There are other people involved, and they could also get hurt."

"Truth is truth," I told him, "and nothing built on a lie ever stands. I promise, Jace, I'll be there for you, and I'll help any way I can."

He nodded. "I have to think about it a little longer. As soon as I have a plan, I'll call you in." He reached over and tuned the satellite radio to a boy-band station, just to tweak me.

I left it there to tweak him back.

GPS coordinates took us past Coquitlam and onto unpaved trails to a field littered with floodlights, white tents and vehicles.

"Smart. Cops can't track them in a field, there's no cell service, and the gang can change location anytime they want." Jace parked his BMW, then put his hand over mine as I went to unlock my seat belt.

"First, my rules," he said.

"I brought you on board—"

"Look around." He squeezed my hand as he spoke. "This place is crawling with drugs, violence, testosterone, and it's all about men punching the crap out of other men." Jace smiled, but again with no joy. "I'm an expert at three out of those four things. This is dangerous for me, but it's fatal for you. This isn't the place to channel your inner ninja or Charlie's Angels. For the next hour, you're mine."

"But—"

He turned the engine back on. "My rules or we leave now, and you never find Amanda."

Seriously. Like I hadn't ever had to live by my wits.

"I'm asking you to do this to keep both of us safe. Can you do that?" He grinned. "Can you dial back your usual kick-ass style and channel it in another way and protect me?"

I laughed despite myself. "How can I say no to that pitch?"

"Good." He stepped out of the car.

I unbuckled my seat belt and stepped onto the grass.

"For tonight, we're dating in the way these idiots see a relationship." Jace came around the Beamer and draped his arm around me. "Don't talk back to me.

In fact, don't talk." He pulled me close. "If anything goes wrong, there's a knife in my jacket pocket."

"If anything goes wrong, there's one in my sock."

He grinned. "No wonder I'm dating you."

I rolled my eyes. "Take us in, Romeo."

"Which tent do you figure?"

I took in the scenery. Smaller tents were scattered in a half circle around a large black tent. "The bigger tent. Looks like the smaller ones are for other things."

We walked toward the main entrance, which was guarded by a beefy guy with sunglasses.

Jace nodded at him.

I did my best to look brainless and awed at the same time, which was a lot harder than it seemed.

"You got the entrance fee?" asked the bouncer.

To add to my pretend airhead act, I threaded my arm through Jace's, pressing myself close like I was impressed by the wads of cash he was taking from his pocket.

Jace handed the bouncer several large bills. His grip on me tightened, and he walked us through the door. The smell of blood, tobacco and sweat filled the space.

I started scanning the crowd, then stopped when Jace gave me a sharp but subtle elbow to the ribs.

"If you're going to do that," he said in my ear, "try to look more curious and less like a cop searching for a perp." He paused. "Do you have a photo of Amanda? Text it to me."

All the bodies had jacked up the heat, and I could barely hear Jace for all the screaming. I shook my head. "I don't have one. Wasn't much for keeping visual records of the people close to me. You know, in case *she*"—I didn't want to use Meena's name—"ever caught me."

"Good point."

"Amanda's tall, thin. Long blond hair, blue eyes."

He raised an eyebrow and tilted his head toward the crowd. "Half the women here fit that description."

I shrugged. "I can draw you a picture."

"No time for that. Point her out if you see her."

The tent continued to fill. After a bit, a guy who had spent too much time in a tanning bed stepped into the middle of the dirt-floor ring. Welcomed the crowd. Reminded them bets were final. He then announced the warm-up event—two girls. Neither of them was Amanda.

I didn't want to watch their bare-knuckle fighting, but if I didn't, it would give us away. So I forced myself to cheer and holler, call for blood, as the girls were forced to bash each other for the crowd's entertainment. When it was done and the smaller girl had fallen, a couple of mouth-breathers dragged her away. The other girl got to do a victory lap while some of the crowd tossed money at her. When she walked out of the ring, a couple more mouth-breathers ran to collect the cash. She'd never see the winnings. All the money would go to the gang. She was lucky they were feeding her.

The announcer stepped back into the ring, announced another fight. This time with two guys. If I'd thought the girls' fight was brutal, this was a level of cruelty I hadn't envisioned. No rules. No time-outs. No mercy. The weaker fighter went down in a cloud of dirt and blood.

"Terminate!"

"Terminate!"

Beside me, Jace froze. I did too.

The announcer walked into the center of the ring. "You heard the crowd. Do it."

Jace reached out and squeezed my hand. I squeezed back until I thought I'd break his bones. He pulled me close. Pressed his face into mine. To anyone watching, it would look like we were getting hot and bothered by the blood lust. But it wasn't about boy-girl stuff.

"Be strong," he said in my ear.

"You too."

We pulled away and forced ourselves to watch what was about to happen.

The winning fighter went over to the fallen man as the crowd surged to its feet.

We did too, because it would have looked weird if we didn't. The people in front of me blocked my view of the ring. Which meant I didn't have to see what happened next. I'd been in flophouses when kids had OD'd, had flipped open the covers of cardboard boxes and found the icy surprise of dead eyes. Exposure hadn't taken away the horror. And being forced to cheer and holler when I wanted to save the fighter was a special kind of torture.

A final blow drew the shrieks and screams of the mob and brought me back to reality.

I whooped and clapped and saw the winner head out of the ring. No victory lap. He just left the ring, not looking up.

The mouth-breathers dragged the body away with all the ceremony of garbagemen hauling out the trash.

Until now I'd thought the kids had died by accident. I hadn't realized they were being forced to kill each other.

"This is new," I said to Jace. I didn't need to say any more. The stakes had been raised for both the gangs and for us. They'd have to find fresh meat. We'd be dealing with more bodies. Jace and I exchanged a long look. The operation had just escalated from dangerous to deadly.

NINE

There was a break in the fight lineup to give people a chance to place more bets or collect their winnings. Jace and I wandered the perimeter, taking note of the security—a knuckle-dragger stationed every twenty feet, with sunglasses, dark blazer and a bulge that could only be a gun. I also took note of the number of exits and weak points. As I was scanning the crowd, checking to see how many of them were carrying weapons, I caught a flash of blond hair and the distinctive movement of my friend.

Amanda.

When she was a kid, her father had come home after one too many at the bar and tripped over a toy she'd left in the hallway. The aftermath of his discipline had left her with a limp. Tonight her limp was more pronounced, and her right hand was bandaged at the wrist. Fight injury. So much for her savior taking her away from a life on the streets.

He was a caveman, beating his chest and dragging her back to the Stone Age, and he swaggered ahead of her. Oil-slicked hair, fluorescent white teeth. And a gym-toned body. He fit the description I'd gotten on the street.

Amanda walked in his shadow, a couple of steps behind. Head down. No eye contact. Whatever this guy had done to her, breaking her will had been top of the list.

I nudged Jace and nodded in Amanda's direction. He squinted at the guy with her, then opened his mouth, but I didn't need him to tell me the obvious. This guy was the boss. It was apparent from the way he walked and scanned the crowd, and the way everyone deferred to him.

And that meant we'd have to leave Amanda. If we tried to take her now, we'd be swarmed. That wouldn't be just totally stupid. It would be certain death.

"Stand over there," said Jace, pointing to his left. "I want to take a picture of you."

Smart guy. I moved to the spot he indicated.

"Smile, baby," he said in a tone only a certain kind of boy used for his girl.

I swallowed and did what he asked.

He took the photo, and I came over to take a look. "Good idea," I said. "Having me stand in front of them. Did you get a good shot?"

He nodded. "Time to get out of here."

We walked away, and with every step I got madder. Mad at the goons forcing kids to beat and kill each other. Mad at the morons who watched it all and called it sport. Mad at the parents who were such terrible people that their kids thought life on the street was better than staying home.

By the time we got to the car, a hot, pure rage burned through me. One way or another, even if I had to break the law, I was going to avenge all the lost kids trapped in this hellhole.

* * *

Jace sent the photo to Bentley. By the time we got back to the palace, he had already hacked into Vancouver's street-camera system.

"It will take a while," said Bentley as we came into his room—filled with enough gadgets to make Batman jealous—and sat down beside him. Three TVs were positioned along the wall. One was tuned to the business channel, another to the news, and the third showed some singer dressed in plastic wrap. Bentley had the volume up on all three sets. The bass of the song competed with the news of the Nasdaq, while a reporter talked about a rash of 9-1-1 prank calls.

I tuned them out as Bentley started to fill us in on his progress. "In 2009, Vancouver got $400,000 to install more than a thousand closed-circuit television cameras all around the city. Since then they've expanded to—"

"We don't need an exact count," said Jace. "Or the history lesson." He looked over at me. "Which, knowing my brother, would inevitably turn into a rant on the infringement of our civil liberties."

Bentley rolled his eyes. "Make fun of me all you want, but you know I'm telling the truth. Big Brother is everywhere, watching our every move. However, in this case, all that surveillance works to our advantage.

"Hopefully, the facial-recognition software will help us zero in on our target. But if that doesn't work, we can use cameras from other businesses. Banks, for instance. Their cameras point out toward the streets, so we can see passersby and other things, like cars and maybe even license plates. Once we get our guy, we can start tracking his movements. From there, it's just a matter of time before *I* figure out his identity."

I know when a guy wants to hear *thanks*. I gave Bentley's shoulder a gentle squeeze. "Thanks, buddy. I appreciate it." I turned to Jace. "And you too. Thanks for the help."

"Anytime." He followed me to the door, where he grabbed my arm and added, "We'll get her back."

Yeah. I just hoped it wouldn't be in a body bag.

* * *

The next morning I texted Bentley to see if he'd had any luck. I knew he hadn't—

he would have passed on stuff as soon as he got it—but I didn't want the mystery man to fall in priority. I heard a beep and saw his reply.

CHILL

Easy for him to say. Hard for me to do. Truth was, after I got a bit of Raven's help to play Spider-Girl and do some wall climbing, I was going to ice out the group on this project. It was too much to ask them to wade into this battle. The field where the fights were being held was an open location, and there were too many things that could go wrong. And there weren't enough of us to set it right if it did. What I needed was a SWAT team, an army, and I knew exactly where to find it.

* * *

"No sunglasses?"

"Would you believe it's out of respect?" I set my bag on the counter.

"No," said Clem. "I believe you want a favor."

"Ouch."

"Truth hurts, kid." He fixed me with an unblinking stare. "I trade favors for work. Help the kitchen make breakfast, and maybe we'll talk."

"*Maybe?*"

"I'm mysterious that way."

I went to put on a hairnet and apron, then got busy frying eggs. Three hours later I wiped the last dish dry and went back to Clem. He was in the office, going over paperwork.

"You still want my help?"

I nodded.

He set down his clipboard. "Then walk away. Whatever you're planning, it's ill-thought-out and dangerous."

"I thought you said you'd help."

"I said *maybe*, and I *am* helping. I'm giving you advice. Take it. Whatever you're getting into is dangerous."

"You don't know that." I looked away as his stare cut through me. "Okay, so it's dangerous, but with your help it might not be so bad."

"This has to do with Amanda?"

"And Ian."

Clem sighed. "Kid, how many times do we have to go through this? Forget about her. You'll only bring trouble on yourself."

"I need your help on this." Because I knew I could trust Clem, I added, "I found Amanda."

He went still.

"The day we went to the coroner, I realized the kids, they were dying because of—"

"Fights." He heaved a sigh. "Specifically, the underground fight ring. Yeah, I saw that too."

"I did some digging, and I found out where the gangs held the last event." I didn't bother to tell him I had a description of the head guy. Knowing Clem, he would dismiss it as too vague. Then he would tell me I was wasting my time.

Clem's eyes flicked my way. "Tell me you didn't do anything stupid. Like put yourself in danger and go there—"

"I just had to check. To see if Amanda might be there."

He groaned. "Your loyalty to that girl is going to be your undoing." Clem went back to his work. "You need to stay away. Whatever's going on, it's dangerous. You-ending-up-in-a-pine-box dangerous."

"I won't end up in a pine box," I said.

"How do you know?"

"'Cause I know you." I grinned. "You'll spring for oak."

He snorted.

"The group is keeping the kids hostage." I moved close to him.

"And you know this because…?"

That made me roll my eyes. "Because if kids were suddenly showing up on the streets or in hospitals with injuries, the coroners would've known what killed Ian."

He shook his head. "Supposition."

"Deduction," I corrected him.

"She made her choice—"

"Gimme a break, Clem. You think she's choosing to stay there?"

"No," he said. "I think she made a series of regrettable choices, and now someone has chosen for her."

I ignored him. "The fights are in an outdoor location. It makes it harder for the cops to track them—"

"But not you."

"These are kids," I said.

"And you're not?"

"You're just going to let them die or be beaten into burger? When you know you can do something? When you can step in and save them?" I asked.

"I've been protecting and serving since before you were born, kid. The first rule of war: don't get attached. Sometimes you have to let some fall in order to save others."

"Is that how you lost your leg?" I stepped closer and got in his face. "Running away from those who needed your help the most?"

"I knew a private like you," he said. "Idealistic. Determined. Resourceful."

"And?"

Clem leaned back in his chair. "They gave him a nice burial."

"Those kids never had a choice," I said, "and you know it. They grew up hard and lived harder. They fell through the cracks—"

"So how come you're not there?" he challenged. "How did you escape the cracks? You know how to jump high and long?"

I didn't answer.

"Tell me you didn't suffer as much as they did." He swiveled off the chair and stood. "You and those kids are the same. You just made a different choice."

"Maybe," I said, "or maybe I'm just stronger. Maybe the wind shifted that day, and instead of pushing me down a crack, it blew me to the side. Who cares? They need our help."

"So you have motivation to help them. What about your weaponry?"

"Minimal." It hurt to admit that.

He let silence do the talking.

"I know it's dangerous—"

"It's not dangerous," he said. "It's a suicide mission."

"Not if you help. You're military—you have ways."

Clem stepped back. "I've given you all the help you're going to get. Get out of the way of whatever this is, kid, and don't look back."

TEN

Bentley found me in a park in Richmond, watching the sky.

"I shut off the phone," I said. "How did you track me?"

"Lowjack on the Porsche."

"And here I thought you lent it to me out of friendship."

"Gotta keep track of you. You're the only art forger I know." He sat down and handed me a Starbucks cup, steam rising from the lid. "It's your favorite kind," he said. "Not from a garbage and hot."

I laughed and took the drink.

"When you didn't come back, I figured it was bad news," he said.

"My contact won't help."

"But we will." He took my hand.

"I can't risk your lives."

Bentley made a sound in the back of his throat and shook his head.

"What?" I asked.

"I see the resemblance between you and Jace now." He ran his fingers in a horizontal line along his forehead. "There's a similarity in the slope…very arrogant."

"Hey!"

"Truth hurts," he said.

"Only when it's true," I argued. "Which it isn't. I don't think I'm better than anyone else—"

"Neither does my brother."

"I'm trying to protect all of you."

"So is he," said Bentley, "and it's frickin' annoying. What do you think? You're the only one who has the skills to fix this?"

"No, but—"

He tossed out the next question. "Oh, I get it. You're the only one with skin in the game?"

"No, but—"

"You're the only one who knows what she's doing," he finished.

I didn't answer.

"Nothing to say?" Bentley asked.

"You keep interrupting," I said. "Thought I'd wait it out."

He grinned and took a swig of his drink.

I took a breath and considered his points. "Okay. If you tell anyone what I'm about to say—"

"You'll make me sleep with the fishes?"

"I'll take away your candy," I said.

"That hurts more."

"You guys…" The words caught in my throat. "You're the closest thing I have to family, okay? I can't risk you or Jace or Raven. If I fail, it's one thing. But if I'm responsible for you getting hurt, arrested or killed…"

Bentley took my hand. "You're not responsible for anything. Look how great we are when we work together."

I chewed on his words.

He laughed.

"What's so funny?" I demanded.

"I just thought of your contact, how he'd feel knowing you were willing to risk his life but not ours."

I punched his arm. "Don't be a smartass. He's had years of experience and military training. The three of you are new to this and—"

"We're just a bunch of kids?"

"No, you're a bunch of rookies," I said. "What's Raven going to do? Swing in on a vine and sweep up Amanda?"

Bentley's lips puckered. "Wouldn't that be something to see?"

That got us both laughing.

"You ever wonder why politicians visit schools?" asked Bentley.

"To prove they can walk without dragging their knuckles on the ground?"

"Because they know kids are the most powerful thing out there," he said. "Think about it. A kid can't vote, but the politician goes into the school anyway, 'cause she knows something. If she does it right, the kid goes home and tells his folks about this great lady he met. And *boom*, the parents are influenced to like her, to vote for her." Bentley stood. "Never doubt if kids can change the world," he said. "They're the only ones who do."

I took the night to think about what he'd said. The next morning I contacted Jace, Raven and Bentley and let them know I'd need their help again. Bentley's software had done its job. It had not only found the mystery man, but also, after Bentley paired the name with a location algorithm, his place—an apartment building in the Bidwell block.

Finding his actual pad would be harder, but for that I had Raven. "We're going climbing," I told her when she picked up her cell.

"Where?"

"Yaletown," I said. "Beach Crescent. Bentley's software found the building of the guy who's keeping Amanda, but finding out which apartment is his is going to be harder."

"Why?"

"For one, the building has a doorman and a front desk. No way we'll get past the doors," I told her. "For two, Bentley's done enough."

"And what's the plan?" she asked.

"Rooftop stakeout."

"What?"

Back to the one-word questions. "You scale one building," I said. "I scale another. We watch the windows, see which one he shows up in."

Silence.

"Raven, are you there?"

"I am. Are you? Or have you fully lost what little sense you were given?"

Before I could get a word in, she continued. "I'm not letting you climb alone.

And playing Peeping Tom with the hope this guy shows up in a window frame is a waste of the night."

"Not with this guy. He's all about showmanship. Trust me, he wanders around with his curtains open. And knowing him, he's on the top floor. I just don't know which side."

"But you *don't* know him," she said.

Crap, she was annoying when she got literal. "You know what I mean. Knowing *his type*. You see a guy like that ever wanting an apartment underneath someone else? No way. He's got to have the top floor. Which means he's a show-off. Trust me, his apartment windows are bare."

"No." She said it like the word had cost her money. "That doesn't matter. You're not good enough to climb alone."

I was, but I wasn't going to get into a pissing contest over this. Raven had lost a friend because of climbing. It hadn't been her fault—she hadn't been there, but that didn't matter. She was terrified I was going to plunge to my death, and I wasn't going to grind her on it.

"Maybe not," I said. "So climb my section with me, and then come get me when we're done."

There was silence. "Come on, *girlita*. The building's all glass and metal, with just the right amount of cement. Tell me you don't want to scale that bad boy."

"Newb. I could use some airtime anyway."

We met up at the Starbucks on Davie Street, then walked the rest of the way, doing our best to stay out of range of the closed-circuit cameras.

But just like with Jace, I noticed Raven looked tired. And like she was walking with a two-hundred-pound weight on her back. "What's going on?" I asked. "Problems with Emmett?"

"Of course I have problems with him," she said. "He's a guy. Their job in life is to make it difficult for us girls."

"So...business as usual?"

Her mouth pulled into a worried frown. "Not really. Remember that girl who jumped off the bridge?"

I did. Raven had seen her on the bridge earlier that same night. The girl had run off but Raven couldn't shake the guilt of knowing that she'd returned to finish the job. "Yeah. Still having nightmares about it?"

"Yeah, except I'm awake," she said. "I think there's more to the story. Something bad's going on, like kids-are-in-danger-and-the-adults-are-responsible bad. My gut tells me drugs are involved."

She would know. Her parents had been giant meth heads. "How can I help?" I asked.

"I don't know yet, but when I do—"

"I'm on board," I promised her.

We walked on in silence and a few minutes later got to the base of the building.

"Ready?" Raven tried to sound casual, but I could hear the fear in her voice.

"Yeah, I'll do everything you say."

She nodded.

Away from the public view, we changed shoes and brought out the dust. I covered my hands with the white powder, then stepped back and let Raven do her thing. While she tied her hair back and dusted her hands, I gently prodded the still-tender spot on my ribs just under the heart. The tattoo was an infinity symbol, a reminder of the endless possibilities that lay ahead of me. And the people I cared about.

Raven stuck her fingers in the cracks between the bricks and hoisted herself up. Then she shoved her toes against the brick and began to climb. There are no safety wires, no toe clips for this. There are only wits and concentration. I followed, keeping a respectful distance. Soon the streets were far below us, though I could still hear the whir of tires on asphalt and the occasional honk of a horn. It took a long time, but we got to the top of the building and hauled ourselves onto the roof.

"This girl, Amanda—she's special to you," said Raven as we sat down.

I pulled out a pair of binoculars and started scanning the windows. "Yeah."

"Don't get all vocal on me about it. The details and backstory are overwhelming."

I resisted snapping back with a witty reply. "She took me under her wing when I first hit the streets. Without her, I wouldn't be here."

"So now you're returning the favor."

"Something like that." Amanda had taken a couple of beatings meant for me, and a couple more because she wouldn't give me up. No way was I going to leave her to her captor.

"Fair enough." Raven stood. Stretched. "I'll head to the building on the other—"

"Hold on." I adjusted the focus of the binoculars, then handed them to her. "Far right condo. That's him."

She took a look. "Nice body. Too bad he's a skeez and definitely too bad he likes rubbing himself down with baby oil."

"Gimme."

"Hold on. I'm scouting...He's got a balcony." She handed the binoculars back to me.

"Get Bentley on the phone," I said.

She did and handed me the cell.

"Can you pull up the floor plans of the Strathford building? The guy's on the top floor and facing west, in the far-right loft. See if you can cross-reference the address to get his name and maybe a bit more background." I shut the cell off after he agreed. "That's the best we can do for now. Let's head back."

* * *

The next day I swung by the kitchen, begged Clem for help and got another no. On the bright side, Bentley had come through with some results. But it was a good news, bad news type of situation.

The apartment was leased by a shell company, which was owned by another shell company. The shell game twisted into a confusing maze of companies, false names and nonexistent CEOs. It was still going to take him days to find out who really owned the apartment and what this guy's name was. Bentley figured the man must have a criminal record and offered to hack the police systems to expedite the process. I knew he could do it. But I didn't like the idea of our using their databases. If they tracked us, it would be over. Permanently.

While Bentley did his part, I did mine. It was easy enough to do some old-school detective work. Late in the day, when the pavement would be full of people heading home, I took a jog past the building. Made sure I wore my blue sweatshirt, hood pulled over my head, dark yoga pants, forgettable shoes—it was all about blending in and being invisible.

I stopped to take my heart rate near the door so I could eavesdrop on people entering and exiting the building. That got me some names, thanks to the helpful doorman, who greeted the building residents as he opened the door and made sure to chat them up. Doyle, Murphy, Rossi. The list went on, but all I needed was one.

"Good afternoon, Mrs. Jansen," said the doorman as he opened the door of a cab and an old lady emerged. Tall, with coffee-colored skin and a mass of short snow-white hair. "How is your knee?"

"Terrible," she replied. "Good thing I'll be getting it fixed. Don't think I can stand the pain much longer. I'll need a car for tomorrow morning."

"What time?" asked the doorman.

"Around ten. I have another doctor's appointment."

I jogged around the corner, then headed to Vincent's place.

"You," he said when he opened the door, "have perfect timing. I just made some—"

"Cookies. Chocolate chip by the smell of it."

"Ayup," he said. "But only good girls who paint get any."

"Aw, c'mon." I doffed the hoodie and tossed it on the kitchen table. It was the only place that wasn't cluttered with Vincent's knickknacks. "I came here to do my own work. I need a canvas and paint."

His silver eyebrows rose in his lined face. "You got a commission?"

"Sort of. I also need the equipment for IDs."

He sighed. "What kind of trouble are you in?"

"The best kind," I said. "I promise. Nothing low or cheap for me. I have self-esteem, y'know."

"My stuff first. Then yours."

"Fine." I scowled. "How long will it take?"

"As long as it takes. Plus cookies."

I pulled a paint smock from his closet. "Who am I impersonating today?"

"Gilbert Stuart," he said.

"The guy whose piece sold for almost eight million at that British auction house?"

"The same." Vincent left me alone to prep the canvas and mix the paints. When he returned, he had a glass of milk, oven-warm cookies and a gummi multivitamin.

"You know I'm not four, right?" I said, popping the gummi in my mouth.

"I go by your emotional age, not your chronological one," he said. "Paint."

I did. And finished off two batches of cookies.

Once the canvas was drying, Vincent sat down to chat. "Tell me about your commission. Who are you forging?"

"Edward Mitchell Bannister."

He gave a low whistle. "I love his stuff."

"Me too." And I hoped Mrs. Jansen would as well. I painted into the night, then slept on Vincent's couch. The next morning, after a quick shower and a raid of the closet Vincent kept for me for suitable business attire, I was ready. Ready, that is, after Vincent had stuffed me full of a hot breakfast and a couple more multivitamins. I promised to check in with him, then headed back out with the canvas tucked under my arm.

When the building was in my sights, I tapped the Bluetooth hooked on my ear. "Bentley, you there?"

"I'm everywhere," answered Bentley. There was a clicking of keys, then, "Ready?"

"I'm waiting for the perfect moment."

"Try to distract the security guard for at least five minutes. I need him concentrating on something other than his console."

At precisely 9:50 I approached the building entrance. "Got a package for Mrs. Jansen," I told the doorman and held up the wrapped canvas.

He nodded and let me in.

I headed to the security guard and repeated my mission, hoping I sounded confident and cocky.

"Sure," he grunted. "Leave it here."

"No, sir, not that kind of package. This one I'm to deliver to her personally."

"I don't have anything here about a personal delivery," he said.

I pulled out the ID card I'd made the night before. "Bridget Hannigan, Vancouver Art Gallery," I said. "I'm supposed to deliver this painting by Edward Mitchell Bannister to Mrs. Jansen."

The security guard folded his arms. "You leave it here."

This was the tricky part. I had to play it with just the right amount of snark to put him in his place, but not so much that he would kick me out. The gamble started with a patronizing smile. "You're not an art lover, are you, sir? Edward Mitchell Bannister's works hang in the Smithsonian. You don't just *leave* his art in a cubbyhole."

"Young lady, I don't care if this painting was by Rapunzel—"

"You mean Raphael."

He glowered. "Whatever. I have my orders."

"Just a couple more seconds," said Bentley in my ear.

I shrugged. "No problem. I'll go back to the gallery and tell them you refused to let me in. And then my boss will call your boss and explain how Mrs. Jansen missed receiving the work of one of the premier artists of the nineteenth century. One whose works were largely ignored in his day because of his ethnicity." I gave him a minute to connect the artist's background with Mrs. Jansen's, then went in for the kill. "Isn't Mrs. Jansen due for knee surgery this week? Think she'll appreciate having to hobble to the door when I have to come back? And how will your boss feel about you inconveniencing an old lady?"

I saw the flicker of indecision in his eyes.

"It's done," said Bentley. "I have control of the building, including the elevators, cameras and the telephone lines. You can move to phase two."

"I understand your dilemma," I said to the security guard, reducing the snark level just a bit. "You have a job to do. But so do I. Perhaps you could call Mrs. Jansen?"

The security guard picked up the phone and dialed. "She's not answering."

"She's in the elevator," said Bentley. "Get ready."

"Let me try one more time," said the guard.

The elevator doors chimed, and Mrs. Jansen appeared.

"Oh, there she is," I told him. "I'll just give it to her now." Before he could stop me, I ran over to the woman. "Mrs. Jansen?"

She nodded and smiled.

"My name is Bridget," I said, making sure the guard couldn't overhear. I pulled out the ID. "I work for the Vancouver Art

Gallery, and I have a gift for you from an anonymous admirer."

"Me? An admirer—at my age?" She laughed. "Sweetheart, you must have the wrong Mary Jansen."

"It's by Edward Mitchell Bannister—"

She gasped. "Oh! I love his work."

"Yes, ma'am." I unwrapped the piece carefully and showed it to her.

"His landscapes were breathtaking."

"Yes, ma'am," I said. "I see that you're on your way out. But perhaps we can make a quick trip back upstairs? I'd feel better knowing it was safe in your apartment."

"Oh yes. Of course. We can't have it sitting in the lobby."

Adults are amazing. If I had told her what was really going on—that I needed to access the condo of a guy forcing kids to kill each other for his amusement, she would've freaked out. Had me kicked out. Probably arrested too. But when I tell her an unknown person has given her a priceless art piece, suddenly we are besties. No wonder email scams work so well—nothing like getting something for nothing to make people drop their guard.

"Oh dear," said Mrs. Jansen. "I just remembered. I have a cab waiting."

"It won't take long, I promise." I hit the button and guided her back into the elevator.

"You're right," she laughed. "The world can wait for Edward Mitchell Bannister."

We rode up together, and I walked her to her door.

"Have a good day, ma'am," I said, handing her the painting. "I hope you enjoy it. If you don't need me for anything, I'm going to take the stairs. I smiled at her and planted my alibi. "I need the exercise."

"Thank you so much, young lady. I do wonder who my secret admirer is." She giggled like a schoolgirl as she closed the door.

I connected with Bentley. "Keep an eye on the elevator. I figure I bought myself a few minutes, but that cab won't wait long."

"I heard every word," he said. "You have to move fast. I can delay the elevator, but I don't want to stop it for long with an old lady inside."

I took the stairs three at a time to get to the jerk's floor. In front of his door, I pulled out a bunch of the gear Bentley had given me and used it to check for surveillance. Then I picked the lock.

"Faster, Jo."

"I'm going as fast as I can. Maybe you should upgrade your tech."

"Don't talk bad about my tech," said Bentley. "If you don't want the security guard wondering why Mrs. Jansen's in the lobby and you're not…"

"Yeah yeah." I pulled out a bunch of pinhole cameras from my bag, stashing them in various parts of the apartment. Then I dealt with the jerk's laptop. With Bentley's help, I ran a backup of his computer drive.

"Everything downloading okay?" I asked Bentley.

"All good," he confirmed. "I stalled the elevator as long as I could. Now get out!"

I raced out the door and ran down the stairs. With all this gear in place, I hoped to get the full scope of this guy's operation. And maybe discover whether he occasionally brought Amanda into town. If he did, maybe I could figure out a rescue plan.

I exited the stairwell just as the elevator pinged. A quick nod to the security guard, and I was racing back to Bentley's. Within a couple of hours, thanks to the information downloaded from the jerk's computer, we had his name: Jimmy Dushku, a top player in the Vëllazëri gang.

The gang and I had a history. They'd worked with Meena—correction. Meena had worked for them. The gang was behind my family's destruction. No surprise they'd be behind Amanda's disappearance and Ian's death too. They had to be taken down, and I was just the girl to do it.

Bentley worked his usual magic and we got the background we needed: multiple charges for assault, human trafficking, drugs, links to terrorist organizations. Now came the "fun" part. Monitoring him. We split into six-hour shifts.

By the time Raven took over from my first shift, I was ready for a shower and a combination ear-eye disinfection. "Brace yourself," I told her. "The man kisses his biceps more often than a mother kisses her newborn."

Day two, I arrived to find Jace staring at the screen. "Did you know he likes to do a before-bedtime workout? In a Speedo?" He grimaced. "Hashtag: Things I'll Never Unsee."

A few days later the mind-numbing surveillance paid off. Bentley and I were sitting around eating popcorn and eavesdropping on Jimmy's life. And I heard what I needed: the location of the next fight.

"I'm outta here." I tossed the bowl of popcorn on the table, stood and reached for my jacket.

"Wait! We should let Jace and Raven know," said Bentley.

"We should also floss twice a day and avoid sugar," I replied with a meaningful nod at the bowl of Skittles and M&M's. "How you doing on that one, Bentley-Bird?"

"They should know," he said and gave me a dad glare. "And don't *ever* call me that again."

"I'm not stopping you from telling them. But I'm not waiting for Raven to disengage herself from Emmett or for Jace to find a shirt that brings out the bronze flecks in his eyes."

"You know he has bronze flecks?" Bentley grinned. "I bet his doctor doesn't even know that."

I ignored him, grabbed his cell and tossed it at him. "Better yet, call 9-1-1. Let the cops know what's going on."

He grasped my hand. "Where are you going?"

"To watch the takedown. Amanda will be there, and I can get her some help." I gave him a hard hug, then sprinted out to the car. After I plugged the address into the GPS, I took off. One way or another, I was bringing Amanda home and finding justice for the fallen.

ELEVEN

It took longer than I thought it would to get out of Vancouver. As soon as I got onto the highway, I hit the gas. The fight was off Highway 91, in the Delta Nature Reserve. I approached the coordinates. There were no tents, no lights, no people. In the split second it took for me to realize that the location was a fake and I'd been set up, my rearview mirror caught the high beams of a truck. Before I could do anything, I heard the sound of metal scraping against metal, felt the harsh *whack* of the vehicle smashing into mine.

Then my car was rocketing off the road and barreling into the ditch.

*   *   *

The airbag cushioned the impact. Sort of. It wasn't so much a soft pillow as a hard slap of air. Dazed and nursing what was probably a broken nose, I fought with my seat belt. But my brain and my fingers were fuzzy, and it took longer than I wanted. Especially given the bruisers heading my way. Two guys, each with a neck the size of my thigh. There was only time to do one thing. I opened my phone and deleted the apps Bentley had created.

One guy tried the door. And when he realized I'd been smart enough to lock it, he yelled something at the second guy. What he yelled became apparent when the second guy pulled a police baton out from behind his back.

I got myself out of the restraint just as he took the baton to the window.

Glass broke into pebble-sized pieces and rained on the seat. I stumbled over the console, unlocked the front passenger door and took off running.

I didn't like the idea of going into the forest, but meeting up with a bear would be better than anything these guys had in store for me. The adrenaline racing through my system made me forget my injuries from the crash. I figured they'd have guns and decided to run in a zigzag pattern. Make it harder for them to hit me. Of course, running in the dark with all the grace of an unhinged buffalo while hopped up on fear and hormones was great. But it was nothing compared to the V-8 Hemi storming my way. Headlights lit the ground ahead of me, not that it mattered. With a rev of his engine, the driver used the front bumper to clip me. The last thing I remember was going down hard and my head bouncing on the ground.

TWELVE

I awoke with a colossal headache, in the kind of wired kennel used for large dogs. It had a blanket and a pillow. And a bucket. The kennel stood in a line with dozens of other cages. Across from me, more wire prisons. The tops of all of them were covered with tarp. We could see each other, but we couldn't see up. The lighting was crap, but I recognized the shape of the person in the container next to me. "Amanda?"

"Josie?"

I tried to reach my hand through the bars, but the slats were too close together.

All I could manage was a couple of fingers. "Yeah, honey. I'm here."

"Oh my god—Jo." She grabbed and held my fingers, then started to cry.

"What happened?"

"Only me being stupid, as usual. I should've listened to you. Should've known it was all too good." She gave a watery sniff. "You'd think with all my experiences with guys like Larry—"

That had been her last pimp. A caveman of a guy who'd still have her if he hadn't OD'd a few months back.

"—I'd have better radar."

"Shh, honey, no point crying."

"But I thought I could trust him. Jimmy seemed so nice and...good. He seemed like such a great guy, but—" Her voice dropped so low I could barely hear her. "He's crazy. Like, insane."

"Forget him. We're going to get out of here—I just need you to stay calm, okay?" I paused a moment and then asked,

"How are you?" I held my breath and waited to hear about beatings…or worse.

She went very quiet.

"Amanda?"

"Terrified," she said. "We all are."

Me too. We needed to get a plan together. "Talk to me. Where are we?"

She gave a dark laugh. "Hell."

"Amanda, focus. I was knocked out. I couldn't track our movements in the car. Unless you give me more to go on, I can't get us out of here." I waited. Waited some more. "Amanda?"

Finally, she answered. "He moves the fight location every time."

"What about this place? Is it new? How long have you been here?"

"This was the first place they took me," she said. "The fight locations move, but our prison doesn't."

Good news: the longer you were at a location, the more of a footprint you left. Bad news: the fact that this location was secure enough to be home base meant they had probably blocked cell signals somehow. Or there was something unique about this spot that ensured no one could find them. It was underground, maybe, or reinforced with concrete.

"Jimmy'll give you a few days," she said. "To get...comfortable. Then he'll make you fight. Bad things happen if you don't."

The way she said that made my skin feel like a thousand insects were crawling over it.

"After the fight, they'll take care of any cuts and injuries," she continued. "The girl-on-girl bouts are popular, and they want to keep the regular fighters around for as long as possible. So they'll be good to you." Another dark laugh. "You wanna hear something funny? Between the food and the vitamins, this is probably the best care my body's had."

"Till they make you fight."

"Like I said, they have meds and doctors." She shifted, her form shadowy in the dim light. "Letting you go is a last resort."

"They're killing kids."

"No, my dear."

I jumped at the male voice overhead.

"Jimmy," whispered Amanda.

"The kids are killing each other," the voice declared.

I let go of Amanda's fingers, went to the cage door and craned my head up. No one was visible, and the echo in his voice told me he was using speakers. Which meant the room was set up with video cameras and microphones so we could be monitored from a separate location.

"Who are you?" I asked.

"Your new best friend. I think you girls have had enough time to chat, don't you? I let you have rooms next to each other—"

"You call this a room?"

"I can always provide other accommodation," said Jimmy.

I went quiet.

"Good girl. Now. Scoot back from the metal. Wouldn't want anything to happen to you."

Something in his voice—twisted delight—kept me from challenging him. I scooted back and took a spot in the center of my cage. A second later I heard a sharp click, then the crackle and hum of electricity as it thrummed through the bars. Amanda was right—we were never getting out of hell.

THIRTEEN

Jimmy doused the lights, and the space went pitch black. No source of natural light meant no windows. With my focus now on my surroundings, I realized the floor seemed to heave and move under me. So we were on a ship. No wonder they hadn't moved location. If the ship was out of port, there was no one to track them except the coast guard, and they had enough to do without random spot checks across the ocean.

And now I knew why we hadn't been able to find Amanda. She hadn't been on land. That's why her phone had last been used on the beach. She'd probably dropped it when they grabbed her.

I lost track of time. The shuffle of kids slipping under their covers eventually quieted to a creepy silence where I couldn't even hear them breathe. I tried to stay awake, and fear was the best kind of caffeine. But eventually the exhaustion took over, and I fell into a restless sleep.

FOURTEEN

A sudden sway in the ship jolted me awake. I heard the whir of mechanics and frowned as my senses told me we were going down. How was that possible? A dull *thud* sounded as we stopped moving. Geez. These guys didn't mess around. The cages must be in a bigger storage container. Maybe a shipping crate. And they'd hung it up in the air. Even if a kid could escape the kennel, they'd never survive the fall to the ground.

I heard the metallic *ching* of a lock disengaging. Footsteps sounded, and soon two black boots—military—came into view. And stopped in front of my kennel. They were followed by more black boots. Then the sound of multiple cages opening, ceramic bowls hitting cement flooring.

I crawled to the door, careful not to touch the bars, and looked up. The tarp on top of the cage made it difficult to see much.

"Get back."

That voice. Jimmy.

"Why?"

"A girl who likes to challenge the guy with all the power, huh? We got a live wire, boys," he said, then turned back to me. "I like you." He sounded amused.

And interested. I swallowed the revulsion rising in my throat.

"But we don't have time right now for your curiosity, kitten. Get back so I can feed you." He crouched, giving me a view of chiseled jaw, dark eyes, thick hair.

"I'm not hungry."

"You'll eat."

"Because?"

"I'll hurt Amanda if you don't." He said it matter-of-factly, and I knew he meant it. And that he'd made good on the threat before.

"I'm suddenly famished."

"Good kitten." He smiled and waved me back.

I did as instructed.

Jimmy looked over his shoulder and waved. There was a loud *click*. The electricity being turned off. He unlocked the door and slid a plate at me. "Eat." Another smile. He sat, yoga style, in front of me.

I took the plate. Roasted chicken. Mashed potatoes with garlic. Grilled asparagus and squash. For sure, there was bad stuff in the food—valium or speed— but the smell was tempting.

"Go ahead." He smiled again. "Eat."

I glanced at Amanda.

"It's safe," she said. "They need us to fight."

"Did I say you could talk?" Jimmy asked her.

She flinched and bent over her food.

I took the fork and reached for the potatoes.

"No." He was enjoying bossing me around. "Eat the chicken first." He held his thumb and index finger a few inches apart. "Little bites. I want you to enjoy your meal."

I did. Then, as I went to take a second bite, he told me to take some potato. That's how the dinner went. Me eating according to his instructions, he clearly enjoying the control he wielded over me. As I continued to eat, the other members of the gang left. And then it was just me, him and the rest of the imprisoned.

"That was nice. Our first meal together." He waved me closer.

A power move to show he was so strong and secure he didn't care how near I got to the door of my cage.

"Time to earn the dinner you just ate," he said.

"You want me to fight on a full stomach?"

His smile was predatory. "You fight when I tell you to fight."

I shook my head. "I'm not beating up some girl."

"Like I said, a live wire. I like girls with charge. Especially smart ones. You ate for Amanda. You'll fight for her too."

"I'll eat for her. I won't beat up one person to prevent you from beating up another."

"What if it's more than a beating? What if it's her life that's on the line?"

Now it was my turn to smile. "We're all dead anyway."

Jimmy laughed. Slapped his thigh. "He told me that's what you'd say."

He? Who was *he?* No way was I going to ask. I'd just have to play along and hope he'd drop the name.

Jimmy wagged his finger at me. "You and me? We're going to have a lot of fun."

"I doubt it."

"Come on, kitten. Get up, and let's go."

"I'll just wait for the cops, thanks," I said. "Phoned them before I left for the park."

"You're cute, you know that? Smart, gorgeous. The whole package. I guess being that hot takes time, and you haven't had a chance to watch TV." He smiled that creepy smile and continued. "Didn't you hear about the swatting that's been going on?"

"Are we talking mosquito season? 'Cause you lost me," I said. I knew what he was talking about, but I needed to delay him as long as I could.

"Swatting. Making prank 9-1-1 calls. There was a bunch, and all of 'em claimed to be the location of illegal fighting rings."

Crap. This was not going well. "Fine. Scratch the cops. I have backup—"

"Your little buddies? They're not coming for you, kitten." He reached back and pulled out my phone. "You're sentimental, and that's your downfall. You should never have saved those texts from Amanda, 'cause now I've got a record of how you talk."

Stupid. I had been smart enough to delete the texts from Raven, Jace and Bentley, and I had been smart enough to delete Bentley's apps. Too bad I hadn't been smart enough to delete the messages from Amanda.

"I've got all your adorable little slang here at my fingertips." He typed in a code, and I heard the click of the phone opening.

How did he manage that?

He thumb-flicked along the screen. "Your friends—"

"I don't have any friends."

"Give me some credit, kitten. I know how to find the ones you love."

My skin went cold.

"They got a text from you. The location was a bust, you said, but you did manage to find Amanda. You're at the hospital with her now, and then you'll be with the cops. And you'll be offline for the next few days."

"And in a few days?"

"Oh, another text. Still with Amanda. Taking time away." He grinned. "It'll go like that for a while."

This could actually work in my favor. Every time he used my cell, it would ping off the cell towers. Which meant Bentley could track me. Maybe I wasn't so stupid after all.

Jimmy scrubbed the underside of his jaw. "Learned from my mistake with Amanda. Lost her phone. If I still had it, I could've been texting you. And no one would have been the wiser." He wiggled my phone. "I'm nothing if not a fast learner. Now it's time to get going. The fans are waiting."

"I told you, I'm not fighting."

"Take a look at all these cages," he said, waving an arm in a wide circle.

I didn't look. Just stared him down.

"I got seven girls here right now. I'll make you a deal. For every six fights you do, I'll let a girl go free on the seventh. Here."

He pulled a small piece of cardboard from his pocket. "I even made you up a card like those coffee shops do. Six punches"—he laughed—"and the seventh's free."

I looked at the card, at six tiny images of boxing gloves. Amanda had called Jimmy crazy. But the time and care this guy had taken to make the card, the fact he had cut off Ian's fingers…Jimmy had gone past crazy and landed in the world of deranged. And, lucky me, it looked like I had prime real estate in his kingdom.

"You're precious merchandise." Pivoting, he swept his arm around the space again before adding, "But these kids. You could save them. And if you don't help, we both know where they'll end up."

"Oh boy. You must be new at this," I said. "Trying to blame me for their deaths is as stupid as those shoes you're wearing."

"He totally undersold how feisty you are."

And another reference to *he*. Had I been wrong the whole time? Was there someone even higher than Jimmy?

"How about this?" Jimmy suggested. "You fight. And I don't kill your friends."

"Told you—"

"What are their names?" Jimmy pretended to think. "Raven, Jace and sweet little Bentley? Think they can survive a sniper's bullet?"

That stopped me.

"Good. You're thinking. That's a smart kitten."

I swallowed. "I have no guarantee you'll keep your word if I fight."

"True. You can't guarantee I won't kill them if you fight, but I *promise* I *will* shoot them if you don't." He grinned. "In the back of the head. Sever the spine from the body. Quick and painless." He sat back. "I'll use a small-caliber bullet, so they can have open-casket funerals. Then again," he said into the silence, "I could just catch them and use them for other things. Bentley, for example. He'd fetch a handsome price. You wouldn't believe the money some people will pay for a—"

"Stop!"

He leaned in. "What do you say, kitten? Do we have a deal?"

FIFTEEN

"Not that I don't trust you," I said, "but I don't trust you."

Jimmy laughed.

His constant grin was unnerving. The guy was a lunatic. But also so arrogant it would never occur to him that he ever had anything other than complete control. I had to figure out a way to throw him off his game. "I'm still not doing it."

"Think I won't honor our deal?"

"I think you'll just replace those kids with others. I think you'll kill my friends 'cause you like killing." I leaned back, faking a calmness I didn't feel. "I think no matter

what deal I agree to, you'll find a loophole."
I smiled. "I think I'm not fighting."

He didn't like that. I could tell by
the way his jaw tightened. "Well, I think
you're wrong. You'll fight."

"This conversation isn't just circular.
It's boring." I scooted away from the
opening. "Lock the cage on your way out
and shut off the lights, would you?"

"Whatever you say." He locked my
cage, then moved in front of Amanda's
and wrenched open the door. "Get out,"
he commanded.

"Stay there," I told Amanda.

"I'm sorry, Jo," said Amanda as she
crawled toward Jimmy. "But you don't
know what he can do."

I crouched to get a better view.
Amanda climbed out of the cage and
stood beside Jimmy, shaking.

"Here's your choice," Jimmy said to
me with a sneer. "Come out and play with
me"—he grabbed a handful of Amanda's
hair—"or I play with this one."

Logic said he'd hurt us both. Logic said that my giving in meant he would torture and torment us. But logic was nothing compared to the memories of Amanda and me.

I moved toward the door.

SIXTEEN

Jimmy tossed a zip tie my way. "Tie your hands."

I did, but in front of my body. He either didn't notice or didn't care. But I did. Having my hands in front of me—even if they were tied together—still gave me a fighting chance.

"I appreciate the jewelry, especially on our first date," I said. "But I have no intention of running."

"We'll see."

He didn't bind my feet. I wasn't sure if that meant bad or even badder things for me.

"Ready?" Jimmy asked.

"Like, totally."

He pushed Amanda to the side. "Step out."

Because of my height—five foot nine—I had to duck as I crawled out. Which was why I didn't notice the needle until I felt it in the back of my neck. I jerked, then rolled crab style away from him and the cage. "What the—!"

"Just being careful." Jimmy had stepped a safe distance away from my feet and fists.

I struggled to stand. Whatever he'd given me, it was fast-acting. My brain may have been full of pudding, but it was still working. As Jimmy grabbed me and hauled me to my feet, I wrenched myself free. And since time wasn't on my side, I went for a low blow. Literally. I kneed him as hard as I could in the crotch.

I grabbed Amanda and pushed her to the door. "Go! Go!" We ran through the exit of the container and stumbled into a warehouse of some kind.

"My vision's going blurry," I told Amanda. So was my speech. "Where's an exit?"

"What?"

"An exit!" I slipped, and she caught me.

Holding on to me with her unbandaged hand, she pushed me in the correct direction. "Left. Run left!"

I twisted free of her. "Go! I'll follow!" I let her go ahead of me. Tried to blink away the blurriness and was glad to see that all three of her were running in the same direction.

Amanda slammed to a stop. "Clem! Oh god, Clem's here!"

"That's fine." I did a slip-slide-stumble to her, then pushed her to keep going. "I told him all about this. He must have been keeping tabs."

"No, Jo, you don't understand—"

"Clem!" Since Amanda wasn't moving, I stepped—tripped—around her. Squinted at his form and what seemed to be a weapon in his hand. "Take her first."

He came toward us. "Didn't I tell you this was stupid?"

"Yes, but—" I shook my head, trying to clear the thickening fog. "Bu...but..." I couldn't remember what I wanted to say. Couldn't seem to get my legs to stay upright. I wobbled. Shoved Amanda in his direction. "Take her. I get him." My words were slurred.

I heard Jimmy behind me, sounding as though he were underwater.

"Are you totally stupid?" Clem asked.

"That's not nice," I said.

"Don't point that thing at me—" Jimmy pushed Clem.

I couldn't see what Clem was pointing, but I hoped it was something with an electric charge or a sharp end. "Point it," I said to Clem, my words sliding together. "Keep pointing it."

"Didn't I tell you to be careful with this one?"

Clem's question, coldly spoken, cleared some of the fog from my brain.

But not much. Not enough. I shook my head, then shook it again. Nothing was making sense.

Amanda grabbed my hand.

"Lecture me later," said Jimmy. "Take care of them now."

"I should take care of you," said Clem.

"What?" said Jimmy. "I covered my bases."

"You should have covered more. You better forget about having kids after that kick she gave you."

"You were spying on me? With the videos?" Jimmy—all four of him—swung toward Clem.

"More like watching over you. I told you she was trouble. Told you to take care. But you're so arrogant," Clem said. "If you'd tied her feet as well as her hands, we wouldn't be in this mess."

Betrayal is like adrenaline. It clears the brain and clarifies the mind. And everything was suddenly making horrible sense.

"That's what I was trying to tell you," Amanda whispered. "Clem is Jimmy's boss. He's the one behind the fight club."

SEVENTEEN

"She's resourceful and smart. And she's working with a team," said Clem. "You moron. You think they're not tracking her?"

"But—"

"Get out of here. And take Amanda with you." Clem sounded disgusted.

Not half as disgusted as I was. I had been so blinded by my trust in Clem, I had never even considered how well the description of the ringleader fit my onetime friend.

"I'll deal with her." Clem grabbed my arm. He turned to me. "I *told* you," he said angrily. "I told you to stay out of it. That there was nothing but heartache here."

"*You*? The whole time it's been you running the fight ring?" I tried to wrench myself from his grip, but the effects of the drug left me sluggish. "How could you?"

"It's a living." He gripped my arm tighter, hauled me a couple of steps, then swore. "He doped you?"

"Didn't want her trying anything." Jimmy paused mid-stride.

"Why are you still here?" Clem demanded.

"Because you're talking to me," Jimmy answered. "You said she was smart. It's not that high a dose. It would have worn off by the time the bell rang."

"She's useless to fight tonight," Clem mumbled.

"So? Send in the blond one," Jimmy shot back. "Maya or Mariah—whatever her name is."

"She's injured."

"So? She can still fight," Jimmy said.

"She's a crowd favorite, you moron. We can't risk losing her. Take Madison or Emily." Clem gestured to Amanda and me. "Tomorrow these two both go in the ring. Tonight—" a torturous pause "—leave them alone." Then he turned back to me. "I told you to forget about Amanda. Told you that you'd only bring trouble on yourself," he said, hauling me back toward the kennel. "You should have listened to me." He shoved me inside and slammed the door shut. "Enjoy the rest," he said. "It'll be the last time you ever sleep here."

EIGHTEEN

I spent the next hour so freaked out it felt like my stomach was trying to eat itself.

"Change of plans," said Jimmy as he hauled me out of the cage and handed me over to two goons. "Clem wants you."

I glanced over at Amanda's kennel. Still empty. "Where's Amanda?"

"Never ask a question you don't want the answer to."

"Thanks for the lesson, Captain Obvious," I snapped back. "You gonna answer or not?"

"Clem took care of her."

"What does that mean?" Even as I asked, I dreaded the answer.

He laughed. "You're smart, kitten. What do you think it means?"

"I think it means I'll be the last thing you and Clem ever see."

"You going to kill us?" He sounded amused.

"That's too good for you. But by the end of the night I'm going to blind you, break you and leave you both for the cops." I kicked and twisted, but my hands were still zip-tied in front of me. Plus it was a fight of me against two mouth-breathers. He and his goons hog-tied me, but they didn't cover my head. So when they carried me out, I had a chance to see where we were. Port of Vancouver, with a clear view of Canada Place. Not that seeing any of it mattered. For sure they were going to move the ship.

We drove in silence to an industrial park, where they hauled me out and dragged me into a trailer. After they tossed me on a couch, they left.

I heard a familiar voice. "Sit there and be quiet." Behind a desk was Clem, staring at a bank of TVs. "This'll be over in an hour, and then we can talk. I don't have time to explain anything to you."

"I don't need your explanations. Don't want them either." I sat at the edge of one of the cushions, glad his back was to me. Stuff always gets dropped in a couch. All I had to do was root around for something sharp that could get me free of my bonds.

"I know what you're doing," he said, his back still to me. "Forget it. I vacuumed the room, the couches and cushions. You won't even find dust mites in there."

"Thanks for the chitchat. It's so hard to sit in silence while kids are bashing each other's brains out for your amusement," I said. "How about some more small talk to keep me occupied while you finish killing a couple of them?"

Clem chuckled. "That's one of the things I like best about you, kid. That mouth."

"What did you like best about Amanda? Hope you told her something nice before you murdered her. It's so sad to die without a kind word."

"Relax, kid, it'll be over soon."

"What did you do to my friend?"

"All in good—what was that?" Clem jumped up as the television screens lit up. He screamed for his gang. In the distance, I heard the chaos erupting.

I smiled as I heard the shouts of men identifying themselves as cops. "I think that's the sound of retribution coming your way."

He wasn't listening though.

Good. Clem was so focused on the screens and directing his band of scummy men, so dismissive of me as a threat, that he didn't hear me as I crept up behind him. Didn't hear as I grabbed the lamp off his desk and smoked him in the head with it. He gave a soft groan and sank in his chair. I grabbed a pair of scissors from his desk and cut myself free. I turned to his motionless figure, the scissors still in my hands, my promise to Jimmy ringing in my ears. Tightening my grip, I moved closer.

NINETEEN

Keeping the scissors at the ready in case he woke up, I took a few seconds to go through the desk drawers, searching for zip ties. I found some and tied Clem's hands together—and none too soon. He groaned awake just as I heard the satisfying *zip* of the tie locking his feet into place.

"What are you doing?"

I ignored his question, unplugged an extension cord and proceeded to tie his legs to the desk.

"Look, kid, you don't understand what's going on—"

"Keep talking. This lamp is still in one piece. Want me to use it again?"

"You're going to regret this."

"Doubt it." I grabbed the laptop sitting on the desk, figuring Bentley would help me extract the evidence I needed.

"It's on OneDrive," he said. "Nothing's on there that can incriminate me."

"We'll see."

"No we won't." Clem sighed. "Untie me and we'll talk this through."

In the background, the *pop, pop* of weapons and the screams of the good and the bad filled the air.

And I smelled fire.

"Hope your '80s dance moves won't fail you," I said. "'Cause you'll have to do some crazy break dancing to get out of here." I stepped around him, laptop in hand. Suddenly the door crashed open.

"Kid!" yelled Clem.

Several black-dressed SWAT cops streamed through the entrance. I didn't know whose side they were on—not really. They could be good guys. Or they could be on Clem and Jimmy's roster, pretending to be good guys.

I had a plan. There wasn't a cop out there I trusted, but there was one person I did.

Raven.

And she was dating the son of a cop. That officer had proven he wasn't all bad. After all, he'd helped Raven out of her mess and made sure the bad guys in the car-theft gang were taken down. He was the only one I'd turn the computer over to. But if these SWAT guys got me, who knew where I or the computer would end up?

Holding the laptop close to my chest, I dropped to my knees, bowed my head and started screaming, "Help! Help me! I'm so scared! They've held me hostage for days!"

They took the bait. As the team screamed at me to get out of the way and zeroed in on Clem, I raced out the door.

TWENTY

Outside the trailer, everything was in chaos. I figured Bentley had used his skills to find me and had then called in the rest of the team. The problem was how to find them without being spotted.

From the red and blue lights of the cop cars tossing color into the night, I could tell the roads were blocked. Which meant my only option was to find a quiet spot in the dark, avoid the K9 unit and wait for morning. It was a cold night, but years of sleeping on the streets meant I could handle getting a little chilled. I ducked low and headed to a bank of trees.

Spotted one with some low-hanging branches. Perfect for climbing. I got myself situated, then watched as the commotion slowly cleared. The night went quiet.

Until I heard the crack of branches under me.

A white spotlight blinded me. I squinted, hoping I could outtalk whatever keener cop had stayed late.

Then I heard Clem's voice. "You can come down, or I can shoot you down. Your choice, kid."

TWENTY-ONE

I opted to climb down. Figured I could stall him until I saw another chance to get away.

"Wondering how I got out of that mess back there?"

"No," I said as I dropped to the ground. "Not even a little bit." Which was not true at all. It was driving me crazy.

"Liar."

"Back atcha, baby," I said.

That made him laugh. "I like you, kid. I really do."

"Does that mean I'm going to live through the night?"

"Your choice." He held out his hand.

I handed over the laptop. "Now what?"

"We go someplace nice and quiet, where we can talk."

Oh man. Everyone knows being moved from one location to another means you're likely to end up dead.

"Don't worry," Clem said as a black SUV pulled up. "You'll have some company."

The windows rolled down.

Jace.

There went any plans of escape.

Jace had enough cuts and bruises on his face to tell me he'd gone more than twelve rounds with someone. Knowing him, a few someones.

"Come on, kid," said Clem. "I think you and I are beyond childish threats." He waved in Jace's direction. "I don't need to tell you what happens if you *don't* get in the car."

I could tell that Jace was in a lot of pain by the way he struggled to open the door.

I climbed in.

TWENTY-TWO

"Isn't this better?" Clem asked, climbing into the front passenger seat. "Warmer, more comfortable—"

"But still with the risk of wild animals preying on me," I said. I turned to Jace. "He do that to you?"

Jace shook his head, then winced.

"Even if I wanted to fight him," said Clem, "I couldn't. Your buddy here was so busy throwing bodies, I spent most of my time doing a duck and cover." He tapped the driver on the shoulder, and the suv started up again. "The child lock's on, so don't bother," he added.

With Jace beside me, too injured to do much of anything, there was no way I could—or would—attempt escape.

"Now what?" I hoped I was still sounding cocky, although I could feel the hope draining out of me.

"Your team messed up the operation," Clem said over his shoulder.

"Well, I'd apologize for messing up your evening," I said, "but I've never been much of a liar."

Clem shot an amused look at Jace. "She doesn't get it." He turned his grin on me. "I'm not sure if I should be insulted or flattered."

"Better explain it to her," Jace answered. "Her words sound light, but I know this chick. In two seconds she'll do some Superwoman laser-gaze thing or go all Hulk. In fact, it's Jo. She'll probably do both."

What the heck was going on? I stared at Jace as he leaned back and closed his eyes.

"If you're going to throw fists," Jace said to me, "aim properly. And Clem, pass me some ice."

Wait a second. My bad guy and Jace were buddies?

"Don't got any," Clem answered. "Hang tight. We'll be in the city soon."

Crap. Those two sounded too cozy for my comfort, but I couldn't believe Jace would ever side with someone who abused kids.

"You look confused, Jo," said Clem. "Let me help."

"Let me guess—"

"I can talk, or you can run your mouth. What's your choice?"

"I'll give you two minutes." I folded my arms. "And you're already at a minute thirty." I stared out the front windshield so I couldn't see Jace. What if I was wrong and Clem had somehow turned him? I couldn't bear to look over at my teammate and see the betrayal in his eyes.

"Then I'll talk fast. Three months and one day after September 11, 2001, Canada and America signed the Smart Border Declaration. The intention was to share more information, to cooperate and ensure the safety of both countries."

"Not that I'm not loving the poli-sci lesson, but where are you—"

"This led to the Integrated Border Enforcement Teams," Clem continued, "and that's basically why I'm here."

"Still not following."

"The gist is this. American law enforcement works with Canadian agencies," he said. "And I'm one of the team members."

"You're working with the Americans?"

"I *am* one of the Americans. FBI. We have intercountry cooperation when it comes to terrorism. And Jimmy Dushku and his gang's slimy fingers are in a lot of bad things. Weapons, human trafficking, drugs. There's evidence to suggest he's funneling the money to terrorist organizations." He scowled at the windshield. "Jimmy's just the kind of bad guy I like to toss down deep, dark holes."

"I'm totally confused," I said, grateful my trust hadn't been betrayed but still reeling from it all. "If you're on the side of the angels, why the stone wall with helping me? You told me to stay away—"

"'Cause you're a loose cannon," he said, his fingers reaching up to touch the growing lump on his head. "Nothing personal, kid, but we both know your situation." Clem turned to face forward but twisted the rearview mirror to catch my reflection. "You and your team are already hiding out from the Canadians. You want to add the Americans to it as well?"

"Good point," I said.

"Besides, I couldn't have you putting yourself in Jimmy's cross hairs."

"Because he was dangerous?"

"Because you'd end him, and then where would I have been? I've got a pension to think about." His grin warmed his words. "Can't have some outlaw kid doing my team's job. Besides, if anything had happened to you, who would share those Wagon Wheels with me?"

"Everything he's saying is true," Jace said, though his eyes remained closed. "Bentley sorted through and verified all of it."

"Bentley's how you found me?"

"He put some kind of tracker on you when he hugged you goodbye."

"Sneaky. But I like it." I kept my tone light, but the truth was, all of this was like getting dumped in wet cement. Then having someone tell me to swim. "I still wish you'd told me all of this," I said to Clem. "I know how to keep a secret."

"I know, kid, but I'd already lost one of you—"

"Amanda."

He sighed. "I tried to warn her off Jimmy, but that girl and bad choices go together like fire and smoke. Once she hooked up with him, I knew what would happen. And I couldn't do anything to stop it." He turned to face me. "I tried to keep her as safe as I could. I promise you that."

"Thanks," I said, feeling a little lighter but still struggling to wrap my head around everything. "Where is she now?"

"In a safe place," said Clem. "Away from Jimmy. Once I got her out of there, I explained everything."

That was all I needed to hear.

"Amanda knows you're safe," added Jace. "Raven too. She told Bentley to tell you that she's found a way in."

More bad guys needing our attention. Bring it on. But first I needed to know how *this* campaign was going to end.

"I can't believe you were an undercover spy the entire time I knew you," I said to Clem.

"Like I always say…" Clem grinned and pointed at himself. "Veteran." Then he pointed at me. "Rookie."

"Yeah, whatever," I said, not quite able to hide my own smile. "What happens now?"

"You want the details, or you just want assurances that Jimmy will be eating through a straw for a long time?"

"How big's the straw?"

"Tiny."

"How much is a long time?"

"He'll forget what solid food feels like."

I settled back into my seat and sighed. "That's good enough for me."

ACKNOWLEDGMENTS

Thanks to my co-authors, Judith and Sigmund, for the good times—the Retribution world is a lot of fun to play in! Also, an infinite amount of gratitude to my editor, Tanya Trafford, whose suggestions amplified Jo's story, and to the entire Orca crew for their hard work and support on my projects.

NATASHA DEEN moved to Canada as a child to escape the racial and political violence of Guyana, in South America. Her books include *Burned* from Orca's Retribution series, *Sleight of Hand* and *Across the Floor*. Natasha lives in Edmonton, Alberta, with her family. For more information, visit www.natashadeen.com.